MEXICAN MERCY MISSION

After Sam's parents and sister are murdered by four bandits in a raid on their Texas homestead, the seventeen-year-old decides to ride south with his uncle, Marshal William Grant. Sam is determined to avenge the deaths of his family members. Across the Mexican border, they talk their way into a fortified hideout with the ambitious hope of rescuing a young girl who has been abducted by the same four killers. And on the way home, pursued relentlessly across the Rio Grande by bandits, they must face one final bloody battle . . .

Books by Richard Smith
in the Linford Western Library:

REVENGE FOR A HANGING

RICHARD SMITH

MEXICAN MERCY MISSION

Complete and Unabridged

LINFORD
Leicester

First published in Great Britain in 2015 by
Robert Hale Limited
London

First Linford Edition
published 2018
by arrangement with
Robert Hale
an imprint of The Crowood Press
Wiltshire

A catalogue record for this book is available
from the British Library.

ISBN 978–1–4448–3696–7

1

Marshal William Grant was about to start his usual evening tour of the town when he saw a lone rider coming towards him through the darkening gloom.

As the youngster dismounted he nearly collapsed through exhaustion but the marshal's instinctive concern was for the animal rather than the human. 'What the hell you playing at, Sam? You know better than to get a horse in that state. He looks like he's about to drop. You rub him down and get him a drink — not too much at first, though. And then walk him round a bit so he cools down properly. I'm surprised at you treating him like that. Shame on you!'

Sam just about managed to recover his breath as he listened to the critical lecture. 'But Uncle, you don't understand. I had to get here as quick as I could. Something awful has happened. Ma and Pa are dead.'

His nephew's gasped words struck the marshal with the force of a prize-fighter's fist. 'What are you saying, Sam? Dead? How?'

'They've been shot. And the place has been ransacked. And our other horses are gone. It was like it when I got back from working in our far field. You've got to come and see.'

'What about Annie? Why have you left her there? Is she safe?'

'I don't know. I couldn't find her anywhere, even though I kept calling her name.'

Although desperately concerned for the safety of his 10-year-old niece, the marshal forced himself to take a pragmatic approach and called across to a bystander who had overheard the dreadful news. 'Bill, please take care of Sam's horse while I get the full story.'

'But we've got to get back there and find my sister,' protested his nephew. 'She might be injured.'

'No, Sam. We've got to be sensible. If you searched and didn't find her, it's no good us going back in the dark. She's probably hiding somewhere. We'll get a few men lined up to ride out with us at first light. We'll stand a much better chance when we can see what we're doing. Besides, you need a rest. Let's get you refreshed so that you can tell me the whole story.'

*   *   *

There were four other riders accompanying Marshal William Grant and his nephew when they arrived at the homestead early the next day.

It was about five miles out of the town of Crown Creek and had been farmed by William's twin brother Brett for the past fourteen years. He had taken it over from their parents when both had died within weeks of each other.

The family had originally arrived in the Texas town when a determined

3

Jason Grant persuaded his wife that, with his two sons growing at an impressive rate, they should have a better future in the developing West.

Though the going was hard, Jason Grant and his wife had established their homestead sufficiently to successfully support themselves and their two boys. One, Brett, seemed well suited to their rural lifestyle, but this was in significant contrast to his brother William, who soon made it clear that crops and livestock had no attraction for him.

Soon after their parents' death, William had told his twin that he was welcome to take total ownership of the homestead while he went into town to earn a living, initially working in a gunsmith's. This, in turn, had led to a life in which he had joined up with an ageing bounty hunter who recognized the young man's wanderlust, coupled with quick wits, a natural intelligence and a kind of inbuilt affinity with the weapons he had been handling in the gunsmith's.

Now the wanderer, William Grant, found himself back in Crown Creek as the town marshal investigating the untimely deaths of his twin brother and sister-in-law, and the apparent disappearance of his young niece.

His first thought as he arrived at the homestead was that the raid might be attributed to the small group of hostile, but increasingly desperate, Indians reported to have still been in the area. These thoughts were quickly dismissed, however, when he saw the bodies of Brett and Debra on the porch where their son Sam had left them in his haste to get into town. Except for the bullet holes, the bodies were unmolested.

'It weren't Indians,' one of the men called out. 'I'm pretty sure they would have put a torch to the buildings,' he continued, diplomatically not mentioning what might have been done to the bodies of the dead husband and wife. 'Will you be taking them into town, or burying them here, Marshal?'

'We'll do it here. Town didn't mean

anything to them, but this place did. But, more important, we've got to find little Annie. I'll search the house if you can look outside. Let's hope she's hiding somewhere.'

In his heart, though, William feared two possibilities: either Annie, like her parents, had been killed, or the raiders had carried her off. The multitude of hoof prints indicated that there had been at least three mounted riders as well as another three horses stolen from the homestead. It was clear that the killers had headed south. The marshal's instinctive inclination was to head off after them but his desire for revenge was tempered by his concern for his traumatized nephew, who now stayed numbly seated by his murdered parents. He hardly responded when one of the men called out, 'I've found the girl. Over here.'

With his heart racing and his hopes raised, William rushed out of the house and quickly covered the few hundred yards to where the man was looking down at his discovery.

'You're not going to like it, Marshal,' he warned as William approached and reached a ditch. In it, lying face down in shallow water, was his lifeless niece with three bullet holes visible in her back. Cradled in her arms was the body of the family dog. It looked as if she had been running away from the intruders when she had been chased and shot down without mercy.

Shocked by the senseless brutality, William yelled just one word as he took in the horrific scene.

'Bastards!' he screamed in anguish.

2

Mindful of the needs of his nephew, William reluctantly resisted the temptation to go in search of the raiders himself. Instead, his deputy led a small posse but they returned after five days.

'Sorry, William,' reported Deputy Jenkins. 'They were clearly heading south but we completely lost their trail when they went over rocky ground that had been rained on. We searched all round but couldn't pick them up again.'

*　*　*

He had never been much of a drinker, but after the deaths of his family members the marshal slid into the habit of having a regular evening whiskey or two in the Lucky Horseshoe Saloon. Three weeks after the murderous raid he was standing at the bar when a young man walked over from the back of the room.

He stood directly next to the marshal. 'You as handy with a gun as folks say?' he demanded.

'What's it to you, stranger?'

'I like to know what I'm up against, Marshal.'

'You ain't up against me, son. Never seen you afore and I hold no grief against you — unless you're thinking of causing trouble in my town.' As he spoke the marshal downed his drink and offered his empty glass to the bartender for a refill, giving the impression that his conversation with the stranger was at an end.

Angrily, the young man grabbed the marshal's left arm and pulled him round so that they were face to face. But as he did so he realized that he had left the lawman's right hand free and he was startled to see that it already held a well-used Colt pointing directly at his stomach.

'So *are* you lookin' for trouble?' asked William.

With no choice, the young man quickly backed down. 'No, not now,' he grunted. 'But I've always wanted to meet the damn bounty hunter who killed my brother in Fort Worth.'

The marshal's face creased into a slight frown as his mind went back over four years. 'I've only ever killed one man in Fort Worth,' he commented. 'And he was a wanted lawbreaker who drew on me first. I had no choice if I wanted to stay alive. I seem to recall his name was Purvis and if you want the truth you had better recognize that your kin only got what he was askin' for, so that don't give you no cause to get involved. Now I suggest you move along and get outa Crown Creek first thing tomorrow. And I mean first thing.'

As he spoke the marshal casually replaced his revolver in its holster, to indicate that their discussion was halted.

For a moment the young stranger

looked as if he was tempted to take things further but he wisely shrugged his shoulders, turned and walked towards the Lucky Horseshoe's batwing exit without speaking aloud. The saloon noise returned to normal when the occupants accepted that the confrontation was not going to escalate into a full-blown battle. It was only later that the bartender revealed that he had heard the youngster quietly mutter, 'We'll see,' as he made his way out.

The next morning Sam was agonizing over the tragic family deaths as he left the Starlight Hotel on his way to the marshal's office, ready for the ride out to the homestead for his first visit since the burial of his parents and sister.

He was familiar with his uncle's habit of patrolling the town last thing at night and again in the morning — always alert to any kind of trouble, as well as visually reassuring the residents that he was guarding their interests.

On this particular morning, William

was especially wary as he remembered his confrontation with Purvis in the saloon the previous evening. His experience told him that he might hear more from the hothead who had come to Crown Creek on a mission of vengeance. The marshal decided that he had better check at the livery stable to see if the young man with a grudge had accepted the advice to leave town at first light, or whether he was still around and likely to cause trouble, even though he had been told that his concept of natural justice was misplaced.

The lawman was walking down the centre of the street towards the stable when he heard the pounding of hoofs behind him on the dry rutted earth. He spun round and was lucky that this action meant the bullet aimed at his back only caught him on the shoulder, though its impact was enough to cause him to twist his body again before falling to the ground.

As his mounted attacker continued to

ride on, the marshal saw another man step from the sidewalk. William immediately recognized him as his nephew, Sam, who stood his ground as horse and rider thundered towards him. Calmly and coolly Sam drew his revolver, took careful aim and fired as the racing roan swerved around him.

The marshal's assailant was dragged along for a short distance before being dislodged from his mount. His body jerked a couple of times when he hit the ground, then lay still as a pool of crimson blood gradually soaked into the dry earth.

When the injured marshal picked himself up and walked painfully to where Sam was now leaning over the inert body, he was impressed to see that Sam's single bullet had accurately penetrated through the attacker's chest. The young assailant who had been seeking to avenge his brother's death was now on his way to an early grave himself.

'Thanks, buddy,' smiled William.

'Those were pretty cool reactions. Your pa will be truly proud of you.' As soon as he finished his sentence, the marshal realized he had used the wrong tense; his brother was dead. The reality was hard to accept.

He felt he was living in a kind of limbo. He had no intention of taking over the homestead himself and Sam had been happy for a neighbour to continue looking after the livestock while he stayed in the hotel, uncertain what to do with his life.

3

The circuit judge presided over a hearing in which witnesses testified that Purvis had tried to kill the marshal and that Sam had acted properly in his retaliation. The marshal had paid for the man's burial out of his own pocket, and he and Sam were the only ones present when a simple wooden marker was positioned to signal the final resting place of a youngster who could only be identified by his surname.

'What a waste of a young life,' commented the marshal. 'He must have been only a kid when his outlaw brother drew on me and it's sad that, without knowing all the facts, his loyalty to a crooked sibling meant that he sacrificed his own life.'

'I feel pretty bad about it, too,' said Sam. 'It was the first time I ever fired in anger, but I thought he had killed you and it was a natural reaction to shoot at him as he rode on. Wish I could have stopped him without killing him, though.'

'Don't blame yourself, Sam,' counselled his companion. 'As the judge said, you were only doing your civic duty when you saw your town marshal gunned down. Young Purvis only got what he deserved.'

Standing silently at the graveside with their partially shared memories, the two men made an ill-matched pair. William Grant was a powerhouse of a man. Tall, broad-shouldered and with a careworn countenance, he had an appearance which had made even strong and desperate men decide not to tangle with him. In contrast, Sam Grant was shorter, slight in stature and some twenty years younger than his uncle.

'What you gonna do now?' asked the marshal, breaking the long silence. 'Will you carry on running the ranch?'

Sam stayed quiet for several more minutes, as if the future was something he had given no thought to whilst grieving for the loss of his parents and sister. Eventually he turned to his companion.

'Don't think so. There's too many hurtful memories there. Anyway, I don't really think that I'm cut out for a life in one place now I'm by myself. Perhaps I'm too much like you, rather than my pa. How about you, Uncle? You stayin' as the Crown Creek lawman?'

'Yep. But only until I hand in my badge. Think I've spent long enough here. Don't want folks gettin' too used to my ugly mug,' he added in a self-deprecating comment.

The marshal hesitated before voicing a proposition that was forming in his mind. 'Sam, I've got a somewhat strange idea, but it might just appeal to you if you're not plannin' on stayin' here in Crown Creek.'

Sam looked up at the older man. 'No, I've made up my mind. I'm movin' on, just like you once did.'

'Well now, son, this might sound crazy but I've had this thought.' The marshal hesitated, seemingly reluctant to put his idea into words. Eventually, he voiced his proposal. 'Well, as I said, I'm plannin' on movin' on myself. Been in Crown Creek too long, I reckon. So I was thinkin' it might be an idea if you and me rode together for a while. Needn't be for long, you know,' he added as a get-out clause.

Sam didn't hesitate. 'Uncle William, I'd be real proud to ride with you. And I'm sure my pa and ma would be pleased as hell to think we were staying together. I know they always felt close to you, even when you rode off with that bounty hunting fella. And I remember seeing tears in Ma's eyes that day we heard you had been injured. Perhaps you'll tell me the story sometime?'

'There'll be plenty of time for that, Sam, if we ride together. Let's shake on it, my young buddy.'

With the legal formalities completed, the marshal handed in his badge and

18

collected his back pay. Unknown to anyone else, he also removed from his office a handful of posters showing rewards of various amounts for wanted men. He reasoned that, on their travels, he and Sam might run across further unsavoury characters who should be helped to find their rightful place behind prison bars, or even on the end of a rope.

He was rolling the handbills together when a stranger came and presented himself at the office door opening.

'Mr Marshal, let me introduce myself. I am Godfrey Pennington-Jones, though most people call me 'the Pen' in view of the fact that I represent the *Chicago Tribune*. I have been sent by my editor to put together despatches about the lawlessness that has developed down here since the war.'

'Really?' was William's guarded response. He had previously had contact with journalists and was not in the mood to accommodate a time-wasting series of questions from a

Northern busybody.

The newsman was not to be easily deflected, however. He was dressed in a strange mixture of Western and city clothes, topped off by a brown derby.

'You know my paper?' he queried.

'Yep. I've seen it once in Kansas City and I weren't impressed. Abolitionist agenda, I recall, and a supporter of Lincoln until John Wilkes Booth put a bullet in his head. So what you doin' down here? Lookin' to run down the South, I suppose.'

Somewhat taken aback, the young man flushed red but had the reporter's determination to press ahead.

'I assure you, Marshal, I only report the facts. I've travelled from San Antonio because I heard you were followed here by a fella called Purvis who was set on avenging the death of a brother you killed in Fort Worth. Can you tell me the story, Marshal?'

'Nothin' to tell. The man was misguided.'

'But what happened, Marshal? Did

the brother find you?'

'Yep.'

'And where is he now?'

'In the ground.'

The reporter could hardly contain his excitement. 'You mean he's dead, too?'

'Yep. Wouldn't have buried him otherwise.'

'You killed him?'

'Nope. You got that wrong.'

'But I'm told he came here intent on killing you, Marshal.'

William replied with a grim smile. 'As you can see, fella, I'm still breathing. Now I've got things to do, so you'll have to do your muck-rakin' somewhere else.'

'But Marshal, this is real interesting stuff. My readers really want to know what's happening down here after the fighting stopped. I guess you fought for the Confederates. That right, Marshal?'

'Told you to git, young fella. My personal history ain't for one of your biased reports, so stop pesterin' me.

Get your pesky questions, your note-book and your unseemly headgear out of here before I lock you up for wastin' my official time that the good townsfolk are payin' for.'

Clearly not satisfied, the newspaper-man continued. 'But I've just been told that you are not actually the marshal of Crown Creek any more. Is that right?'

A somewhat rueful smile crossed the face of the taller man. 'Well, now, I guess you got that much right, fella, but that means you got even less justifica-tion for wasting my time with your pesky questions, so get out of my way. I'm leaving in the morning and I've got no time to waste on you.'

★   ★   ★

'Where we headin', then?' Sam asked his uncle, as Crown Creek disappeared into the distance behind them the following day.

'Well I reckon I've seen a good proportion of this land north of the Rio

Grande but I've never been down into Mexico. How about we head that way?'

'OK with me,' said Sam, not quite believing that his companion was simply riding on a sightseeing trip without a set purpose in mind. For the moment, however, he was quite happy to follow his partner's lead and see where it would take them. He had no premonition of the dangers they were to face as they headed south.

4

Sleeping under the stars at night, by day they rode steadily through increasingly inhospitable territory with much sandier soil and an abundance of cacti. Not far from the border, they reached a farmstead on the outskirts of a small town. Since it carried a painted sign outside indicating that it also operated as a cantina and boarding house, they decided to rest up in comfort for a few days before crossing the river that would take them out of Texas. They found that the place was run by a harassed-looking man who appeared to be about the same age as William Grant.

Although he welcomed them warmly, he seemed to struggle to meet the gastronomic needs of his hungry guests. His only help appeared to be a boy of about nine who eventually brought their food and later showed them to their rooms after they had downed a few tumblers of tequila.

The next day they left their horses stabled and ambled across the small stretch of land which separated the cantina from the main town. Although still north of the border, Plympton had a distinctly Mexican appearance.

Set in haphazard fashion along the central street were a mixture of family dwellings and commercial premises, nearly all of which were in a dilapidated state. Two cantinas were separated by a large church, and William — whose religious upbringing had long been abandoned — pondered how such a small community had found the resources and manpower necessary to construct such an impressive edifice.

A few mangy dogs ran loose or hid away under any shaded area they could find to protect themselves from the sun's already oppressive mid-morning heat. Although some of the men sported the flat-topped hats common in west Texas, there were as many sombreros in evidence as there were Stetsons.

William and Sam wandered into a general store where two long counters were piled high with all kinds of merchandise, much of it looking as if it had sat in the same place, gathering dust, for weeks or even months.

At one end of a counter was an unstructured display of foodstuffs, including sacks of flour, corn and a huge supply of coffee. William bought some sugar, which the innkeeper had been unable to offer them the previous evening, and haggled with the store-keeper over the price of shells. Sam was surprised at the quantity his companion ordered, and took the unspoken hint to make sure he himself stocked up with sufficient ammunition to meet whatever hazards they might encounter on their future travels.

On their return to the cantina there was no sign of the owner, but his son was sitting on the dusty front porch sobbing his heart out. They questioned him sympathetically and got a jumbled story about his mother being killed and his sister being taken away. That evening they teased the full story out of the boy's father. With a voice containing a mixture of anguish, bitterness and real anger, the man said that, about a month earlier, a group of four strangers had ridden in and demanded food, drink and accommodation. It sounded like good business and he had been more than happy to meet their needs.

After eating, the four strangers had settled into a game of cards and consumed copious quantities of tequila. They got rowdier and rowdier and, just after midnight, an argument had broken out, with two of the men squaring up to each other ready for a fight. They were stopped, however, by a few terse words from the oldest-looking of the four, who seemed to be their leader.

The two sat down again sullenly by which time the innkeeper's tired wife had taken the opportunity to start clearing the debris from the table. As she did so one of the men grabbed her and pulled her on to his lap, putting his hand on her breast as he did so. The other three laughed as she struggled to free herself.

Her husband told William and Sam that he had been punched in the face when he went to intervene. Stunned, he had fallen back against the wall and the two men who had been arguing got up and delivered more solid blows to his face and body. When he slumped to the ground, they removed his belt, tore down a drape from the window and tied him to a chair.

He described how he was forced to watch in horror as the two younger men forgot their quarrel and combined forces to start ripping off his wife's clothes, even though she struggled fiercely and managed to stick her thumb into the eye of one of them. The man screamed in agony and threw her to the floor.

Before continuing with his story their host broke down in sobs, which continued for several minutes whilst William and Sam sat in silence waiting for him to recover some degree of composure. Neither of them had seen a grown man shed tears before and they felt some embarrassment at the experience. There could be little doubt that the man telling his story must have led the tough life common to all those who had chosen to settle in the harsh environment of the region and his open display of distress therefore added emphasis to the depth of his agonies.

But he hadn't yet finished his sorry tale.

When he felt able to continue he shocked his guests even more. 'That weren't the end of it,' he choked out. 'When she pulled herself to her feet, she picked up a knife from the table and stabbed it towards the face of one of the brutes. She didn't make it, though, because the other attacker tripped her with his leg. As she toppled back to the ground, he picked up the revolver he had left on the table and shot her three times. She died immediately.'

Again he fell into a heart-rending silence. Eventually William asked quietly: 'What happened next? Your son said something about his sister.'

By now the hostelry owner could hardly speak coherently. 'She heard the shots,' he started, and then fell into silence again before continuing almost in a whisper. 'She heard the shots that killed her mother and came through from the back room where she had been sleeping. As she looked down at her ma the two young men grabbed her and stripped her nightdress off so she was completely naked. Then they held her down on the table and urged the third man to take his turn. He didn't need much encouragement. My poor terrified girl didn't cry out. She just whimpered in shock and pain. She's only thirteen,' he added as the conclusion to his story.

But William wasn't satisfied. 'What happened next?' he asked again. He seemed to be determined to get the whole story, although it was obviously distressing the innkeeper to be forced to recall the terrible incident.

Slowly the man continued with his narrative. 'They took my daughter through to the sleeping area with them. In the mornin' they helped themselves to food and left early. They took poor Carla with them. I could hear her yellin' for me as they rode off. My son, who had miraculously slept through it all, untied me after they had left.'

Again William pursued the story. 'Did you seek help?'

'Yep. I went to the county sheriff, Mike Goodrich, and told him all about it. He sent his deputy out here, and he helped me bury my wife. He carried out a bit of an investigation and confirmed that five horses had skirted round the town and had been seen riding off south towards the river. One of the horses, a black gelding, was mine, so that's what they used to carry poor Carla away.'

'What did the sheriff do?'

'Nothin'. Absolutely nothin'. He just said he'd record it, but told me there was no way he would chase after the men.'

★ ★ ★

When he had calmed down after telling his sorrowful story, Hawkins told his guests that he had originally been an itinerant cowboy who had arrived at Plympton sixteen years earlier. He had stopped at the small hostelry, which was then being run by a frail elderly Mexican couple and their daughter, Maria.

They had employed him to carry out much-needed repairs to their building and outhouses. After years of hard riding, Hawkins had been happy to take life a little easier for a spell. He had stayed longer than he originally intended, helping Maria run the place as her parents' health deteriorated further. After a few months they had both died, and Hawkins had married their daughter.

Although they made little money from the irregular flow of visitors stopping at their place rather than in the town, the couple made ends meet by growing vegetables and keeping chickens and goats.

Glad to have some sympathetic listeners, Hawkins told William and Sam that they had been happy enough. 'We were delighted when we were blessed with the birth of Carla and then our fine son, Anton,' he continued. But he struggled to control his emotions when William returned to the more recent events.

'You say the sheriff did nothin'?'

'No, he didn't really seem all that interested. He said the four men were almost certainly over the border into Mexico by now and there was no point chasing after them as he had no jurisdiction over there. He didn't even seem to care what might have happened to my poor Carla. Heaven knows what those men might do to her, but there is nothin' I can do about it myself when I've got young Anton to look after.'

★   ★   ★

The next morning William surprised Sam by bringing a small bundle of rolled-up papers with him to the breakfast table. He spread them out to reveal that they were reward posters showing wanted men with various prices on their heads, depending on the severity of their crimes and whether the rewards were funded or boosted by interested parties such as banks or rail companies. Some posters featured care-fully executed drawings, whilst others were basic sketches or even just a few words giving little detail of the wrong-doers.

After Hawkins brought their food

William got him to study the posters. The innkeeper carefully scrutinized the first four without any sign of recognition, but when he came to the fifth one he immediately shouted in excitement. 'That's him! I'm sure of it. He's the leader, the one who just sat watchin' and blowin' smoke from his fancy cigar when the younger three attacked Maria and Carla. Look here! It says his name is Rutherford and he's wanted for holdin' up a stage and robbin' the passengers. Says he had a coupla other fellas with him and there's a two thousand dollar reward offered for his capture.'

When Hawkins looked carefully back through the four other posters he failed again to recognize anyone else as those who had killed his wife and abducted his daughter, but he returned to the poster of Rutherford. 'That's him. Stake my life on it.'

To William's delight, Hawkins then started to draw on the back of Rutherford's poster and soon, with a surprising skill, produced passably good illustrations of the other three men. He also scribbled notes about their height, weight and dress. When he had finished, William asked if he could also provide a picture of his missing daughter, Carla.

Lovingly her father produced a new drawing showing a young girl with white skin but Mexican features, with shining dark eyes and jet-black hair down over her shoulders. He also added a distinctive crucifix which, he said, her rapists had left hanging on a chain around her neck when they violated her young body.

'What you gonna do with that information?' Sam asked his companion after Hawkins had left the room.

'Well, first I'm gonna tell that lazy, no-good sheriff how to do his job. He should at least have got Hawkins to provide descriptions of the attackers. Now he can get someone to copy these drawings and get them circulated.'

'And the originals?'

William smiled. 'Reckon we might just keep them ourselves,' he replied. 'Never know who we might bump into on our travels and two thousand dollars is a very handy sum.'

He added nothing further about his intentions, but somehow Sam sensed that there was more than a touch of determined seriousness behind his casual comment. He wondered what his companion was up to, but decided to keep his peace until his uncle was ready to tell him what he was planning.

5

Although not delivered as an actual order, the tone of his uncle's voice was firm enough to persuade Sam that dissension was not expected. 'You stay here and help out a bit while I ride over to Sheerwater and pay a visit to that varmint sheriff.'

When he returned late the following day, William told Hawkins that he would be leaving with Sam the next morning. 'We'll be back, though,' he promised. 'Don't know when, but we'll be back sometime. You have my word on that. Meanwhile you just take care of yourself and that boy of yours. He's had a real nasty experience because of those murderous bastards and will need a lot of reassurance that there's not gonna be more bad stuff to come.'

* * *

When they departed from the cantina, William said nothing about where they were heading and Sam decided not to question him. They were obviously continuing south in the direction of the great river which separated Texas from Mexico, but when they actually reached it Sam suffered a sense of disappointment that, for that year at least, it did not live up to its name. The width of the channel between the Rio Grande's opposite banks was impressive but the actual water flow was remarkably slight.

'Can't have been much rain,' observed William rather unnecessarily as — without consulting Sam — he turned right, to head in the direction of distant El Paso. Sticking as close to the river as possible, they continued to ride steadily for two more days, with the ex-marshal on a course unknown to Sam. Since the older man appeared not to be in a hurry to communicate his intentions, Sam remained curious but held his silence.

After they had made camp on the

following night, however, William produced some written notes and a sketched map. 'Sam,' he said, 'I think it's about time I told you what I'm up to.'

'I'm listening. Knew you weren't ridin' just for the fun of it. What's on your mind, Marshal?'

'Well, first you had better stop callin' me that. You know I handed in my badge, and where I'm headin' marshals aren't exactly welcome.'

'OK. So where are we headin'? You seem to have had something on your mind ever since we left the Hawkins place.'

'Yep, I have, and I reckon I've been a might unfair to you, son, in not lettin' you in on it earlier.'

William paused and Sam let the silence hang in the air. Although he thought it was possibly simply a figure of speech used by an older man addressing a much younger one, he felt pleased by the way his companion sometimes called him 'son'. It seemed to consolidate the family bond which had always remained, even though his uncle had left the homestead long ago for a more adventurous life, before returning years later to take up the role of Crown Creek marshal.

As they sat round the intimacy of the camp-fire, Sam felt brave enough to question his uncle about the reasons for his much earlier decision.

For a while it seemed as if his uncle was to remain secretive about a matter which had never been discussed openly before. After a long pause, however, he decided to open up. Slowly, he started by saying there were several reasons for leaving his brother Brett to manage the homestead. 'First,' he said, 'it's true that I didn't really care for the life of a farmer. And, anyway, it wasn't clear that the homestead would be able to support all of us. Guess that's what you've always been told, isn't it?'

'Yep. That's what Ma and Pa said when I asked them about it — but I always felt there was more to it than that. Did you and my father have a row, or something?'

'No, there was nothing like that. It was more difficult. Now your parents are gone, I think you have a right to know the story. Truth is that I loved your mother. We both did — me and Brett. She was a lovely, wonderful person and we both wanted her. The three of us spent much of our time together but in the end, she had to make a choice. It was so hard for her, for all of us, in fact.'

There was clear emotion in William's voice as he continued to unburden himself. 'She was torn in two. She said she loved us both equally, but in the end she said she had decided to marry my brother. It nearly destroyed me, but I had no choice. I had to accept her decision, even though it meant I had to break from her and Brett so that they could build their lives together without me being there, getting in the way of their happiness. But I never stopped loving her. I've never found any other woman I felt the same way about. Now I miss Debra as much as I am sure you do, Sam.'

William sank into silence. It was a long time before Sam felt able to speak. 'Thanks for telling me that. I understand a lot more now, and I'm so pleased we are riding together. I hope we can stay together for at least a decent time, but I have to ask you what you are planning to do. Where are we heading? I'm sure you've got something in mind.'

'Truth is,' William responded, 'my old bounty hunter instincts came back to the surface when I heard the innkeeper's story and found he was able to identify Rutherford from the posters. There's a good price on his head, and although the money won't hurt me, most of all I want to see if I can catch those bastards and find out what they've done with poor Carla. There must be a strong possibility that they are the same ones who killed our folks. Nothing can replace your sister Annie, of course, but if I can possibly return Carla to her father and brother it will make me feel a great heap better.

'I questioned that lizard of a sheriff pretty hard about where those bandits might have headed. He wasn't exactly helpful at first but he finally told me about a place where they could be. Apparently there's a hideout not far on the other side of the river in the direction of Chihuahua. It is used as a refuge and resting place by all sorts of rogues. It is outside the reach of Texan law so no one can touch them once they are across the river. And the Mexican authorities don't seem too bothered either, as long as the scum who go there don't cause trouble on their side of the border. That sheriff fella says he's never seen the hideout himself but he was able to give me quite a bit of information about it and he seemed to think there were good odds that's where our four bandits have headed with the girl. So that's where I'm plannin' to go.'

'OK,' Sam interrupted, 'but there's one thing puzzles me.'

'What's that?'

'Well, I've just heard you talkin' about your plans but I heard the word 'I'. Aren't we supposed to be riding together as buddies? If you're goin' after these guys, then count me in too. I'm just as concerned about that girl as you are. At least we can bet that's she's still alive, which is more than we can say for Annie. If we could possibly rescue her it would somehow ease the hurt for losing my lovely little sister. I miss her so much, so I know how poor Anton must feel.'

William smiled, and held out his hand. 'Hoped you might say something like that,' he said as Sam also stretched out his hand to consolidate the pact that they would face whatever they encountered as a team. But Sam wanted to know more about what his partner had in mind.

Drawing on his past experience, William said that gangs of lawbreakers sometimes set themselves up in permanent lairs where they could rest awhile before setting off again to rob a bank or undertake whatever their particular unlawful specialism was.

'That sheriff said he had heard from captured bandits that at any one time there could be twenty or more guys holed up there. Apparently they are in some kind of canyon they can defend against anyone approaching. It's only about thirty miles away from the river and is run as a refuge for gangs keepin' away from the law. Sounds like a pretty well organized setup and the sheriff seemed amused that I had thoughts of ridin' in there. Certainly didn't seem to rate our chances of getting the girl out. He says that, unlike many white bandits who are feared and even hated by the Mexicans, this lot maintain good relationships with their Mexican neighbours by buying food and other stuff from them, and by providing them with guns and ammunition.'

Sam interrupted again. 'But if it's

well guarded, how we gonna get in?'

'Well, we sure ain't gonna shoot our way in, so I reckon we'll have to talk our way in,' was the enigmatic reply, provided without further elaboration.

6

They'd crossed the Rio Grande by noon the next day, with Sam still not getting used to the dry, yellow and rocky scene which contrasted with the area he had been brought up in. Following the rough sketch grudgingly provided by the sheriff, they eventually located a flattened trail which led to what was obviously the canyon entrance. There were steep protective cliffs on either side and it was clear that it would be impossible to enter without being seen by guards posted on top.

As they started to ride in there was a rifle shot, followed by a shout coming from behind a ridge.

'Hold up there! Who are you? What do you want?'

In reply, William slowly and deliberately took his Winchester from its scabbard and held it high above his head to indicate that he had no intention of using it to fire back, but — without speaking — he continued to ride on slowly into the canyon entrance. Sam followed his lead.

As they rounded a bend, two horsemen appeared, having obviously been alerted by the earlier warning shot. William and Sam pulled their mounts to a halt and the two guards closed in on them with rifles at the ready.

'Who are you? What do you want?'

William responded firmly. 'Names are Randy and Sam Ross. We were trailed by a posse,' he lied, 'but they didn't cross the river behind us. We need somewhere to hide up for a while until the heat is off.'

'How come you knew about this place?'

'Fella I was with in jail told me about it some while ago,' William replied.

'What was his name?'

'Never knew for certain but he wore

an eye patch and everyone called him Black Eye. He was shot when the three of us broke outa jail.'

The two men conferred for a while, but then decided to accept the story and ordered the two new arrivals to ride on ahead of them. As they rode slowly up the canyon, William quietly confided to Sam that his story was based on fact. There had been a thief and murderer known as Black Eye, and he had indeed been shot while breaking out of jail. 'It was me that killed him,' added William, 'but the other two got away. I heard they headed up into Wyoming. I never got a chance to track them down.'

When they got through the canyon it opened up into a wide flat area which seemed to be entirely enclosed by the surrounding mountains to provide a remarkably secure environment.

William and Sam were impressed by the size and sophistication of the encampment as they approached across a track with grassland and light brush either side of it. It was like a small township set in an oasis within the mountains. There was a cluster of small adobe buildings, with larger ones stretching further out from the centre. Several had their own small cultivated areas around them. To one side was a larger adobe and timber house, with a mesquite corral round it, built almost like a stockade to one side.

A sturdy wooden bridge crossed a narrow river, which flowed down from the western slopes of the high ground and crossed a plateau of grassland on which a number of cattle were grazing. Along the banks of the river were cottonwood and sycamore trees, and mounted on an area of higher ground was a Napoleon smooth-bore gun-howitzer rescued from the Civil War and brought down over the border. It was now pointed at the canyon's opening into the hideout.

The two newcomers were led across the bridge and told to dismount. Their horses were taken by two men who had watched their arrival. William and Sam were then walked to a central area where chopped tree trunks lay on the ground to form a circled arena, which obviously acted as a meeting point. As they were directed into this space, about a dozen men and, surprisingly, a few women, appeared and gathered round.

A tall, thin man led the questioning. Looking completely out of context to his surroundings, he was dressed in fancy city garb. An embroidered brocade vest was worn with a yellow cravat under a dark suit. He was flanked by two men who were obviously professional gunslingers. One was a full-blown caricature of the gun-for-hire mercenary. He was dressed from head to toe in black, right down to thin black leather gloves designed to enhance his image without detracting from his ability to draw and squeeze the triggers of the two revolvers slung low to both his sides. He stood with his feet placed firmly in a set stance, with his hands hanging loosely beside his guns.

The other man also had the drooped shoulders that William recognized as the stance of an experienced gunfighter, but — a little surprisingly — this one was a Mexican *pistolero* rather than a lawbreaker from the other side of what the man would know as the Rio Bravo del Norte.

Neither of these two spoke but their role was clear as they stood firmly either side of the questioner in the fancy duds.

Sam listened as intently as anyone else whilst his companion used his background knowledge as a bounty hunter and lawman to make up a convincing story of how they had been hunted after unsuccessfully trying to rob a stagecoach up in Arizona Territory. According to William, he and Sam (who he accurately described as his nephew) had been frustrated in their attempted hold-up when, by pure chance, a sheriff and two deputies had been riding nearby and had heard the warning shots fired to stop the coach driver.

'They chased us for a while, but then went back and formed a proper posse, which tracked us across country until we got down to the river. Sure was a close call.'

'I still want to know more about how you could find this place,' demanded their examiner.

'Goes back a coupla years,' said William. 'I was jailed with this Black Eye fella who liked to boast about what he'd done, who he'd killed and how much money he'd thieved while operating in Texas. We had plenty of time to talk and one day he told me about this hideout across the river. Said he had never actually been here himself but had ridden with others who had used it when they wanted to keep outa the way of the law. He said enough for me to find it when we came across the river ourselves to escape our trackers.'

Clearly not fully convinced, the questioner wanted to know more about the alleged escape from jail.

'We were waiting for the arrival of the circuit judge. In with me and Black Eye was a fella called Casey, who headed a gang which operated mostly in Oklahoma but had come down South to rob a bank. The way he told it, Casey had been captured when his horse was shot as they made their escape. But his men staged some kinda incident that drew the sheriff and his deputy some miles away from the jail we were in. In their absence, two more of Casey's men overpowered the elderly deputy left to guard us and all three of us escaped. Black Eye got shot by an interfering town busybody. Casey rode off north with his two gang members and I rode south to my sister-in-law's place.'

Seemingly now more convinced by the plausibility of William's story, his questioner moved on to examine Sam.

Quick on the uptake, Sam said his father had been killed after the Civil War by a group of Northern bandits who had roamed the South after the hostilities ended rather than return to their former homes. 'When my uncle came to us after his escape from jail, I decided to ride out with him. It was more excitin' than stayin' with my ma, and my brother was better than me at caring for our small farm, which barely produced enough to keep the three of us alive.'

As if becoming bored by their exchanges, the questioner abruptly turned back to William and delivered his verdict. 'OK. You can stay, but we've got rules. My name's Ian MacDonald. While you're here in Glencoe you do what I say, and you don't leave without askin' me. And don't expect a free ride. What you gonna contribute while you're here?'

William shrugged. 'Don't plan on stayin' long. I've got a bit of cash but we've both got muscles we can use for anythin' that needs workin' on.'

MacDonald turned to one of the men in the group surrounding the newcomers. 'You deal with them,

Dickens,' he said. 'Put them to work on that irrigation channel.'

With his two henchmen either side of him, MacDonald walked out of the arena towards the main building.

Surprised that they were allowed to keep their weapons, William and Sam were led to an impressive bunkhouse and allocated sleep places. The man deputed to look after them then took them to another building where they could eat. After travelling on bare essentials, they were delighted to find the cookhouse offered as much good fare as most eating houses across the Western towns, but with a strong Mexican influence. 'Good job I like tortillas and enchiladas,' muttered Sam as they filled their bellies with large meals washed down with copious quantities of red wine. They kept their conversation as general as possible, aware that their appointed guardian was listening carefully to every word — no doubt with a brief to report back to the man who had introduced himself as Ian MacDonald.

As they downed coffee after their meal, the two newcomers had a good look at their fellow diners; they were amazed at the mixture of people seated around them. Texans and Mexicans predominated but other accents came from much further north than Texas.

There were two Negroes sitting together and, even more surprising, two impressively tall figures Dickens identified as Yaqui Indians. 'They don't say much, and keep themselves to themselves,' he added, 'but MacDonald has apparently had them with him ever since he set up this place. I'm told they were a tribe never conquered by the Spanish but they kinda adopted Christianity into their own culture and that pleased MacDonald, the boss around here. What he says goes, so don't you cross him if you want to stay healthy.'

7

The next morning William and Sam were allocated the task of digging an irrigation trench which led from a stream to an area being prepared as a plot for growing vegetables. 'Sure looks as if they ain't plannin' to quit this place in a hurry,' William said as they sweated at their labours. 'And they've clearly been undisturbed by the law for years.'

Though the digging was demanding, they made good progress until their minder came back to tell them they could take a break.

'I intended to, don't you worry,' said William. 'We're not here as slaves, fella. No one's gonna tell us what we can and cannot do.'

Dickens replied with a grim smile on his face. 'I'm not so sure about that,' he said. 'Anyone who doesn't follow

MacDonald's rules regrets it. He has his own form of justice.'

'Such as?'

'Well, only coupla weeks ago a fella from Montana was caught stealin' from another fella. MacDonald didn't mess about. Got himself a huge sabre and cut off the varmint's shootin' finger, then sent him on his way outa here with only a day's food and water. Like I told you, it don't pay to mess with MacDonald.'

For their afternoon break the uncle and nephew were allowed to wander round unaccompanied. It seemed that either they had been accepted as genuine lawbreakers qualified to use the hideout or — more likely — it was considered that they wouldn't be able to cause trouble, or escape past the guards posted at both ends of the canyon. As they meandered around the compound they assumed a casual appearance but surreptitiously took in as much of the setup and its inhabitants as they could.

'Wish I could claim the bounty money for this lot,' muttered William, as his thoughts turned to his earlier role. 'Make a pretty packet if you could get the rewards for all the rogues in here.'

'Sure,' agreed Sam, 'but we seem to have drawn a blank as far as trackin' down those men who took young Carla is concerned. No sign of them here, so that sheriff was wrong in his guess that this is where they were makin' for and — '

'Hold on, young Sam,' interrupted William. 'Look over there, behind that shack. See that girl hangin' out some washin'? That could be her, couldn't it?'

'You're right. Same dark hair, but it's been chopped. Let's take a closer look.'

Still trying to appear casual, they changed their walking direction slightly to get closer to the girl, but had made a major miscalculation. As they moved to the side of the building, a rifle poked out of a window.

'What you two up to? Get back away

from here or you're sure gonna taste lead.'

'Sorry, mister. Don't mean no harm. Just moochin' around,' replied William to their unseen interlocutor. 'We'll head right back the way we came.'

'Make sure you do — or else!' came a warning from inside the building, and William and Sam didn't hesitate to heed it. Their challenger certainly sounded as if he meant it.

That evening, when they were seated in the eating area used by many of those in the hideout, they were brought coffee by a man they had seen before but had not spoken to. He stood directly opposite William and, without preamble, spoke in a low voice. 'I know you, and I remember that your name ain't Ross.'

For a moment William froze. He prepared to go for his gun, but then relaxed somewhat as he figured that the stranger would hardly be whispering or leaving himself vulnerable to attack if he intended to expose the newcomer as an imposter. Nevertheless, he decided to remain in denial. 'Think you're mistaken, mister,' he said. 'I don't reckon we've bumped into each other before, and I don't think you know me.'

'Yep. I sure do, big fella.'

It was said in a near whisper but was enough to make William wary. Ever since they had ridden into the hideout he had feared that someone would recognize him from his multifarious past and denounce him.

Instinctively, his hand again dropped back down to hover over his .45 Colt as he looked up at his challenger. He was a short, stocky man, but without the weather-beaten face common to most who had lived an outdoor life in the sun. Also setting him apart from most of those in this villains' bolt-hole, was the fact that he was not armed and William was able to discount him as a physical threat. More important, though, was the danger posed by his words.

William stayed silent, wondering

fearfully what would follow from the initial challenge. Reassuringly, though, the stranger continued in a low voice to avoid his comments being overheard by anyone else.

'You had a moustache then, but I know it's you. Can't mistake that frame anywhere. Ain't many built like a lump of rock carved off the side of a mountain. Up in Montana it was. Place called Row Town.'

Immediately, William acknowledged to himself that the man's recollection was perfectly accurate. He remembered the place, and the incident, absolutely clearly. He had perhaps been lucky to come out of it alive. But he wasn't yet ready to admit this memory.

'I ain't callin' you a liar, mister, but I think you're mistakin' me for someone else. I ain't never even heard of Row Town, let alone been there.'

The man was still standing but his head was only a foot or so higher than William's face when he gave out a throaty chuckle, revealing such mal-odorous breath through blackened teeth that his listener involuntarily had to turn his head away. 'I suppose it is just possible I might have got it wrong but I'm absolutely certain that you're the same fella who shot those two varmints that was gonna kill me. Won't never forget what you done for me. Didn't get much chance to thank you then but sure want to do so now.'

William relaxed. Although the man's appearance had aged considerably, he came back from the depths of Grant's memory as the plucky bartender who was defiantly refusing to open a safe placed down below the bar of the small town's only saloon.

One of two would-be thieves had already shot the man in the arm and they were threatening him with his life when William had innocently entered through the batwing entrance into the otherwise deserted saloon.

The details flooded back as if the incident had been hours ago, rather than years. One of the two outlaws had wheeled round and immediately fired at William but his shot had been too hasty and missed by a foot or so before the bullet embedded itself into the wooden frame of the saloon entrance.

In one instantaneous movement William had stepped to his right, drawn his revolver and fired back at his assailant. He had deliberately aimed low but his shot had been dead centre and had gone straight into the man's soft belly. With a yell of pain the man dropped his weapon and clutched both hands to his punctured body as the blood seeped out and quickly turned his hands a sticky red. William vividly recalled the man's stricken horror as he looked down at his wound before slumping to the ground, gasping his last few breaths before heading to the place in hell which was his well-deserved destiny.

Meanwhile his companion in crime had turned his attention away from the barkeeper and was belatedly going for his own gun. He was far too slow, though. Before he had got it out of his holster, his shooting arm had been disabled by William's bullet through the shoulder. This was sufficient to end the contest as the man at the bar surrendered to his superior antagonist.

'Don't shoot, mister,' he had shouted as he raised his uninjured arm above his head.

All this now flooded through William's mind as he gestured to the man he recognized as the barkeeper from that distant past.

'OK, friend. You've got the right man, but you had better sit yourself down and tell me how you come to be here, same as me.'

'Nope, not now,' came the reply. 'We've been seen talkin' long enough and that could be dangerous. Just wanted to let you know who I am and that I still owe you big time. If there's anythin' you need you can count on me. Folk here call me Bert.'

With that he turned and ambled

away, leaving William still ruminating on the distant incident and reflecting on how the past could so easily return to impact on the present.

During the brief exchange, Sam had remained silent. Now he asked: 'What was all that about? Do you think it's a threat to us?'

'No. I'm sure it's OK. Fella really does owe me a favour — though heaven knows how he finished up here.'

8

They worked solidly at their digging for two more days until a messenger came over to say that MacDonald wanted to see them. He led them to the largest of the houses, where MacDonald's two protectors were sat on the porch, placed either side of the door. As William and Sam went to enter, they were barked at by the gunslinger, again dressed entirely in black. He spoke with an unfamiliar accent. 'Clean off those boots before you go in. Mr MacDonald don't like folk messin' up his fancy polished floors.'

Inside they were amazed at the luxury of the room MacDonald occupied. He was sitting behind a huge mahogany desk. Over his shoulder was an oil painting of the man himself, standing against a mountain backdrop and dressed in a kilt. Decorating the walls were a couple of claymores and a stuffed stag's head with huge antlers. MacDonald was clearly proud of his Scottish ancestry.

There was also an extra decorative addition to the room. Sitting in a huge leather chair was the most beautiful woman William had ever set eyes on. Although she was seated, it was obvious she was tall, and slender. She had shiny black hair, probably denoting a Spanish heritage. She was dressed in a low-cut white silk top and black skirt split at the side to reveal expensive leather boots topped by a generous expanse of white thigh.

She sat motionless, gazing at the newcomers with piercing eyes, and William felt an immediate deep sense of connection that he would have found impossible to explain but which impacted on his emotions in a most powerful manner.

MacDonald obviously had no intention of introducing her or explaining her presence, however, as he started in with further questions.

Sam's examination was relatively short. He simply stood by his earlier straightforward, but largely fictitious, story that he had lived with his widowed mother and his brother until his uncle had shown up after an absence of several years. 'Why did you decide to ride out with him?'

'There was no choice, really. Our little homestead couldn't properly support us. It had always been a struggle, even when my pa was alive. But after he died we had two bad crop years in a row and were forced to borrow from the bank. Anyway,' continued Sam, 'I had already made up my mind that I needed to leave so as to make it one less mouth to feed. I was bored silly, too, and my uncle arrivin' was the perfect opportunity to make the break. My ma was worried but seemed happier to let me to go off with him, rather than travel by myself.'

Sam permitted himself a wry smile before adding that his mother didn't know the illegal line of business her brother-in-law operated in.

This comment seemed to relieve the tension a little, but MacDonald still persisted in questioning William about his past.

Again using his background as a bounty hunter and a lawman, the ex-marshal convincingly reeled off a string of stories about robberies and other illegal deeds. What his listeners, including Sam, did not know was that the stories were mostly true but in telling them William transferred his own role from the right side of the law to the wrong side. He became the villains he had actually brought to justice.

After about twenty minutes, during which the two newcomers had been kept standing in front of him, Mac-Donald decided to cut short the interrogation. He nodded at William.

'OK. You're free to go, Ross, but I'll want you back again tomorrow to tell you about a job I've got for you.'

* ★ ★

The next morning the Mexican gunslinger was sat on the front veranda
when William returned to the *hacienda*.
He wondered if the man had been there
on guard all night.

The Mexican did not speak. He
simply jerked his finger to point to
William's boots.

'*Buenos días, mi amigo,*' William said
in an attempt to get some kind of
personal contact going, but the only
response he got was a penetrating stare.
The look in the dark eyes was akin to
the gaze he had seen before in captives
when he had the barrel of his Colt .45
pointed at their chests. Clearly he was
not going to establish any kind of
relationship which would help him in
his quest to uncover information about
the abducted Carla.

In fact, when he and Sam were
together over breakfast, they admitted
to themselves that they weren't making
much progress at all. William said that

his early morning visit to MacDonald had been absurdly short. He had merely been told that he was to wait for further briefing. This time, to William's considerable disappointment, the woman had not been present.

As they sat eating, they noticed that other diners who passed them by were giving them more studied looks than previously, but still none bothered to speak. It was not the friendliest place in the world, Sam commented.

'Guess most of this lot don't want folk prying into their business, Sam. Remember we're still strangers and they have all got personal history to hide. We'll just have to bide our time and keep our eyes open, I guess.'

★ ★ ★

In fact, it was two more days before there was any further development. They were mending a fence when the gunslinger dressed entirely in black came over to them.

'Boss says you've got to come with me and Bert to collect supplies tomorrow,' he said to William. 'Be ready at daybreak. Leave the youngster here.'

Without further comment or explanation, he turned and headed back to the main house.

'I'm guessing that's some kind of test, and you're to be left as a guarantee that I follow orders,' said William. 'But at least it should give me a better idea of how things are organized here.'

It turned out that the man who had been referred to as Bert was, indeed, the one from Row Town who had already made himself known to William and Sam. When they headed out through the canyon, he drove the wagon with William seated beside him.

The man in black rode separately and waved at lookouts hidden in the upper area of the cliff faces. William carefully noted their positions as they returned the greeting.

'Who's our fancy escort?' he asked his companion.

'Calls himself Hank, but that ain't his real name. Been told it's really some kind of English moniker. Apparently he came from some place called Cornwall because he's a mining expert. Came hoping to find silver in the Tombstone area but decided to be a gunman instead. Knows all about dynamite but prefers being a shootist. He's MacDonald's number one man.'

As they drove on, William saw that Bert was following a fairly well delineated track, heading further south. It certainly would not have been difficult for anyone coming in the opposite direction to have found the route to the canyon entrance and the hideout.

'Why is MacDonald left in peace when it's pretty obvious where the route to the hideout is?' he asked.

'Easy. The local Mexicans don't particularly like us, but they do OK out of us. We bring them stuff from over the border and pay them well for the food and stuff we get from them. Mac-Donald's got some system for paying off the authorities, too. Suits everyone to leave us alone. I'm told Mac-Donald's been here for over six years. Although he disappears now and again, he never goes for more than two or three weeks at a time. Story is that he was once an officer with the Union but then made a packet sellin' guns, horses and other stuff to the Confederates. Guess he's got some pretty good reasons for not goin' back over the river himself.'

Keeping a careful note of the dry and uninviting landscape they were travelling through, William took the opportunity to get as much information as possible from his companion, but decided to reinforce the man's apparent loyalty by first giving him a chance to tell his own story.

'How come you're here?' he asked. 'And I don't recall your name was Bert when you spoke at the trial.'

'No, you're right.'

Despite the man's seated posture, William could sense his chest swelling with pride as he confirmed that his name was Alberto Lopez and his family had come from La Laguna in the Canary Islands.

'Canary Islands?' queried William. 'Bit of a funny name. Where are they? Somewhere off the East coast?'

Bert laughed. 'No, no. They are about a coupla hundred miles off the West coast of Africa. Quite a lot of us come from there. Finished up all over the place and practically founded San Antonio. One of my folk died in the Alamo.'

'I'm impressed,' said William, with genuine admiration for this man's illustrious connections with the heroes of that vanquished band of defenders against the might of Santa Anna. 'But what about you? How come you finished up here, servin' up grub to a load of villains?'

'Strange story. Don't really understand it myself. But you'll remember, of

78

course, that you weren't judged guilty of killin' the man in the bar at Row Town?'

'Of course. You testified that he fired at me. His bullet in the wall and revolver on the floor proved that. But what about the other fella? Seem to remember he got away with it.'

'That's right. His name was Rattigan. The judge ruled that, as his gun never came out of his holster, he hadn't done anything wrong. He seemed determined to ignore that the two of them, together, were demanding that I opened the safe. Was something funny about the whole thing, especially when, after the trial, my boss told me I was sacked from my job, even though I had been tryin' to protect his money. Even stranger was that no one else would give me work. Not any kind. It was as if I was the criminal and Rattigan had done no wrong. In the end I had no choice but to use my bit of savings, buy a horse and ride out.'

William pondered this strange story

for a while and hazarded it was some sort of put-up job. 'Sounds almost as if your saloon boss wanted to be robbed and you and me got in the way. Don't understand it, though. I once dealt with a case where a bank manager linked up with a load of bandits to steal from his own bank branch and share the money with him. Could be some sort of scam like that, and you were the fall guy. But what happened to you after that, Alberto?'

'Better not let anyone hear you call me that,' warned his companion. 'It would suggest you know me from somewhere else.'

'OK. You're right. I'll stick with calling you Bert. But carry on with your story.'

'Not much to tell. I wasn't cut out for a life in the wild. I was in a pretty poor state when I was picked up by a gang on the loose. They sort of adopted me to do their cookin' and chores, as well as actin' as a lookout or stooge for some jobs they pulled. Eventually we wound up here. The gang I came in with pulled out about three years ago, but I stayed.' He paused. 'I ain't got anywhere else I need to go, so I reckon this is where I'll be until my Maker comes to claim me.'

9

As Alberto Lopez finished his tale, they arrived at the small Mexican village, which was their destination.

William noticed that when the wagon entered what acted as the main street, those citizens outside quickly disappeared. A couple of children pointing at the man in black were grabbed by their mothers and hustled indoors.

A priest standing in the high wooden doorway of his church half raised his arm in recognition but then, seeming to think better of it, turned and went inside. Clearly, thought William, the wagon's visits are tolerated rather than welcomed by the villagers.

Riding slightly in front of the wagon, their escort stopped in front of an impressive general store. He hitched his horse and went inside.

Within seconds an elderly couple

scurried out as speedily as their ageing legs would carry them. They glanced fearfully over their shoulders before scuttling down the dry dusty street at the fastest pace they had probably moved in years.

As Alberto drove past the store, Hank came out and, legs apart, stood at the entrance, clearly intending that no one would enter.

Alberto, though, guided the wagon a little further on before he manoeuvred it into a narrow passageway between two buildings. At the end he turned right again and pulled up at what was obviously the back entrance to the store. He clambered down but when William went to follow him into the store Alberto stopped him.

'You stay outside. I'll bring the stuff to the door and hand it to you so that you can load it into the wagon.'

Waiting outside as he'd been told, William was first brought a large container of flour. Then for over twenty minutes a steady stream of basic provisions were handed to him — everything from sugar to wine.

After that, Alberto came to the door carrying a large, carefully wrapped container which he handed to William with a stern warning. 'Stack that lot very carefully. It's MacDonald's whiskey. Heaven knows where he gets all this stuff from. I just come and collect it.'

'Who pays?'

'Never been sure. I don't. But Hank goes into the store when I've finished loading up. Perhaps he settles up. Or perhaps MacDonald arranges it himself when he makes his occasional trips out. None of my business, and it don't pay to ask questions. Anyway, let's get goin'. Hank will be behind us and it's best to get back before dark.'

They had driven in silence for about twenty minutes before Alberto suddenly posed a question that he had perhaps been storing up since they had left the hideout. 'So you saw La Condesa?'

'La Condesa? That what she's called?'

'It's what MacDonald said we had to call her — though we hardly ever see her, so it don't much matter. He claimed it was a matter of respect for her aristocratic background. We never knew whether that was true or not, because no one knows her real name or anythin' about her. She arrived about eighteen months ago with two large wagons of stuff. They came with an armed escort who were not allowed through the canyon. One wagon even had a piano, which she plays every night. Fella in charge of bringin' it said it had come all the way up from Mexico City. Seems almost impossible that it got here in one piece. There was loads of other fancy stuff as well. All a bit strange, it is.'

'Strange?' asked William. 'What do you mean?'

'Well, we assumed at first that MacDonald had brought her here as his woman. But one of the two Mexican boys who act as their housekeepers let slip that they sleep alone. Seems one hell of a waste to me that a beauty like that ain't properly accounted for.'

*   *   *

As the sun started to slide down towards the mountains, Alberto suddenly jerked on the reins. '*Madre de Dios*. Looks like trouble ahead — up by that small copse.'

'Yep. I see them,' confirmed William, as he peered through the darkening gloom at three mounted men sat motionless beside the rough trail they were following back towards the hide-out.

'*Bandidos*, I reckon,' said Alberto. 'Looks like they knowed we was comin' this way. First time it's happened on any of the trips I've done. Local troublemakers are supposed to know to give us safe passage. And where the hell is Hank? He's supposed to be protectin' us.'

'Haven't seen him for a while, Alberto, my friend. Seems like we'll have to look after ourselves, and we ain't got too many options. We certainly can't outrun them with all this load on board. We can't turn off the trail because of all the loose boulders, and it's no good just sittin' here waitin' for them to come and get us. Reckon our best bet is just to ride on and face the music.'

'But we're sittin' ducks up here,' complained Alberto.

'I know. So be ready when I shout to jump off your side and get straight down behind the wagon. I'll jump down my side. I'll shoot as I go if that's what's needed.'

Alberto drove on slowly. The mounted men stayed where they were. Then, as the wagon got nearly within rifle range, two shots rang out, but they had not come from the waiting Mexicans. Instead, two of the would-be attackers dropped to the ground, neat bullet holes in the centre of their backs.

The third man's horse reared up at the sound of the shots and that gave the man a chance to turn towards his attacker. It did him no good, however. The only difference it made was that he got his bullet in the chest rather than in his back.

'Thanks, Hank,' shouted Alberto as they drew up to the man in black, who had dismounted to inspect the three bodies. Without a word, he came over to hitch his horse to the back of the wagon, before returning to the corpses.

William and Alberto watched in silent fascination as the man in black carefully removed the bandits' holsters and weapons. Then he dragged the three bodies so that they were carefully lined up side by side with their feet all pointing towards the setting sun.

Next he retrieved the men's sombreros and placed them over their upturned faces. Finally, he folded their arms across their chests so that the three bodies were formed in a regimented pattern.

'What's that all about?' murmured Alberto.

'Don't rightly know,' said William. 'Perhaps it's some kind of respect for men whose lives he's taken. Or perhaps he's just tidy minded!'

Alberto's thoughts were more practical. 'More likely it's intended as some sort of warning to other *bandidos* that they'll finish up the same way if they mess with MacDonald or his supply wagons. Not that those three bodies will stay that way for long when the vultures and coyotes get at them,' he mused, as he watched Hank throw the bandits' weapons into the back of the wagon. William got down from his perch and helped grab two of the bandits' horses. The third had bolted but Hank did not seem inclined to chase it.

He shrugged at William. 'Already got me a bonus from this trip,' he said with something vaguely resembling a smile, before mounting his own horse and riding off to resume his effective protection role as they continued back to the canyon.

As they rode the supply wagon through the entrance Alberto waved and, on either side, got a response from the guards on duty, making themselves visible to return his greeting. Once again, William carefully noted their positions and was fairly certain he could locate them if necessary. He had no firm plan in mind, but felt certain that the guards had to be negated somehow if they were to be prevented from thwarting any escape from the hideout.

10

Soon after William had left with the supply wagon that morning Sam decided that he would return to the building where they had seen the girl hanging out the washing. But as he went round a corner he came face to face with a man he was sure matched the drawing Hawkins had made of one member of Rutherford's gang.

'What you snoopin' around for? What you want?'

Stuck for an answer, Sam decided to tell the truth. 'Thought I saw a girl here earlier,' he admitted. The man grinned. 'And I suppose you were lookin' to enjoy a bit of warm meat. Was just thinkin' about grabbin' a bit meself but I reckon there's no reason why you can't go first. It'll cost you, though.'

Sam nodded and then haggled over the price because he guessed that would be expected. He was ordered to leave his revolver on the table before he was pointed through the door into a room which was really not much more than a box with a bed in it.

The girl sat on it and her face carried a look he'd never forget. Fear? Hatred? Contempt? Probably all of those, as — without saying a word — she started to remove her top.

'Hold on, Carla. I'm not here for that.'

She looked amazed. 'How do you know my name? The others just call me 'the girl'.'

'Don't be frightened, Carla. My partner and me was with your pa and brother. We know what happened to your ma and you and we're gonna try and get you outa here.'

Still suspicious, she asked: 'What was my ma's name?'

'Maria. And your brother is Anton.'

At the mention of her family details, the girl's eyes filled with tears, but she soon turned to practical matters. 'How on earth can you expect to get me out of here? The whole place is like a fortress and I'm watched all the time.'

'I don't know yet,' admitted Sam. 'We've got to work out a way.'

They talked for a while longer, with the girl anxious to hear news about her father and brother. Sam told her what he knew from their brief stay at the cantina. She, in turn, blurted out something of what happened since the four bandits had abducted her and brought her to the hideout.

Seeing tears in her eyes, he reached out and squeezed the girl's hand in a friendly gesture. But this seemed to worry her, as if any form of contact brought her fears back to the surface after the treatment she had received. She pulled her hand away from Sam's touch.

'Be brave, Carla. We'll find a way to get you outa here somehow. But you be brave for a little while longer.'

But when Sam went back through the door he got a reception he wasn't expecting. His weapon was no longer on the table and the gunman was standing to one side with his own revolver pointed at Sam.

'What you playin' at? You didn't do nothin' to her. I was watchin' and all you did was talk.'

Sam realized that there must be some kind of peephole so that the voyeuristic man had been able to watch his meeting with the girl.

'Somethin' funny goin' on, I'd say, when a young fella don't want to satisfy his natural needs. Turn round!'

There was a dirty broken mirror on a dresser and as Sam turned away he could see the man start to raise his gun in order to crack him over the head. What he could also see, though, was Carla come out of the small room with a vicious-looking kitchen knife in her hand. She had obviously kept it as a potential form of protection.

She quickly stepped up to her captor just as he raised his revolver to stun Sam. With a little scream she reached up and plunged her weapon into the man's neck. He dropped his gun and put his hand up to where blood was gushing out.

But the girl wasn't finished with him. She quickly struck again into the man's side. He staggered forward and she struck him once again as her bottled-up hatred gave her strength and determination.

As the man collapsed to the floor, Sam had to restrain her, though he well understood her fury when she looked down at her tormentor. 'He was the one who did it to me at our home,' she panted out before collapsing on to a chair, her whole body shaking.

Her frantic revenge for the indignities piled upon her was a new trauma rather than a sweet release. Even in the tough existence of the American West, killing a man was not something that should be experienced by a 13-year-old girl, Sam reflected as he put a gentle comforting arm round her shoulders. This time she didn't shake him off but clung to him and sobbed against his chest for several minutes before he gently loosened her grip on the knife still in her hand and got her to sit down.

He was aware that the other three bandits could possibly return at any minute and both their lives would be in danger. He was not sure what to do, and desperately wished that his uncle was around to deal with the situation. Though he was worried at leaving the poor girl, he forced himself to accept that he had better not be found at the scene of the stabbing.

Reluctantly, he left Carla and made his way back to the main buildings.

11

When the supply wagon reached the building that acted as the storehouse for the encampment and which MacDonald had named Glencoe, Alberto Lopez dismissed William, saying that others would come and help with the unloading.

He therefore wandered over to the bunkhouse in search of Sam, who he found to be alone, but in a very agitated state. Without waiting to ask about his uncle's trip, the young man launched into a rushed tale of events back at the hideout.

'Just after you left, I went back to where we saw the girl before. It was Carla, all right, with one of the men that Carla's father drew for us. Have you got the papers so that I can show you which one? Where are they? I looked in our saddle-bags but they weren't there.'

His companion cut in to stem the flow of excited words. 'I guessed our stuff would be checked; I've had the dodger posters strapped to my leg since before we arrived.'

Sam, though, was rushing ahead with his narrative, eager to relate the gruesome story of Carla's revenge. 'But what did you do then?' asked his concerned listener.

'What do you mean?'

'Well, where's the body now?'

Sam looked worried, wondering what William was getting at. 'I left it where it was. I didn't know when Rutherford and the others might return and I didn't want them to find me there. I figured it was best just to let them think Carla had acted by herself when she found she was alone with the man who had raped her.'

'OK. But it must be terrible for her to be left with the body and we can't know what reprisals they might dream up when they discover their dead buddy. I think we had better go over and get rid of the evidence.'

★   ★   ★

In the dark they sneaked out of the bunkhouse and went to the small building used by the Rutherford gang. When Sam told Carla that William was his friend and the two of them were working together, the girl hardly seemed to acknowledge their presence.

William decided that something had to be done to shake her out of her apathetic state of shock. He told Sam he was going to take the man's body to bury it where they had been disturbing the earth to repair some fencing and that, while he was gone, he and the girl should clear up the bloody traces of the killing. Then, with one movement, he hoisted the dead rapist on to his shoulder and disappeared into the darkness.

He returned two hours later and found that the two youngsters had indeed managed to clean up all signs of the day's earlier events. William was disturbed, however, to see that the girl was still in a state of shock and he decided he had to be tough with her if she was not to endanger all their lives.

'Listen, Carla,' he said. 'This is important. We don't know when the others will be back but they're gonna question you and it's absolutely essential that you give nothin' away or they might decide to take drastic action against you. Do you understand?'

To his relief the girl nodded as a form of acknowledgement.

'You must say you have no idea what happened to him. You just woke up and he was gone. Do you understand?'

Again she nodded and William softened his tone. 'We're gonna get you outa here and back to your pa. But meanwhile you have to be patient and say nothin' that will give the game away or involve Sam and me.'

* * *

Early the next morning, William was woken by one of MacDonald's two Mexican houseboys.

'You come. Quick,' he said. 'Quick. Quick.'

Fearful at the cause of the panic, William pulled on his boots and followed the boy to the *hacienda*. He wondered whether their nocturnal activities had already been discovered. Had Rutherford and his accomplices returned and discovered the disappearance of Carla's rapist?

When he was stood in front of MacDonald he was relieved to find that his summons was not related to the killing and burial of the gang member.

'I've got a job for you,' said the Scot. 'A man called Rutherford will be back from an exploratory mission later today and tomorrow you're to go out with him on a little hold-up job I'm arranging.'

'What about my nephew?'

'He's to stay. He's a sort of security, if you like. We don't know much about you and I want to make sure you do what's expected of you.'

'But I don't normally work as a member of a gang,' protested William, determined to use this opportunity to find out a bit more about how MacDonald managed the setup and controlled matters from his hideout headquarters.

'Listen to me. You came here seeking refuge. Now you'll repay the debt you owe us. You'll go out with Rutherford and two others. You'll take your orders from him. However many of you get back will share half the proceeds of what you make and the other half goes to me.'

'And after that?'

'Then you'll be free to go if you want to and also be free to return any time you like in future — as long as I feel you've repaid your debt and can be trusted.'

'What sort of job is it you want me to do?'

'You'll find out tomorrow. Remember, you'll take your orders from

Rutherford. OK?'

William nodded his acceptance and turned to go, but a sly leer from MacDonald left him with an uneasy feeling that somehow things weren't exactly straightforward.

Perhaps he wasn't destined to return from the mission with Rutherford?

He decided that some pre-emptive planning might be in order, and that action needed to be taken before he was scheduled to go out with the outlaw. When he returned to Sam he got him to go back to Carla. He was to provide her with his timepiece and tell her to be ready to slip out at three o'clock the following morning.

★ ★ ★

Next on William's action list was a meeting with Alberto.

'You said you would be willing to help if there was anythin' we needed, but I don't want to press you into anythin' you don't want to do.'

103

'It's OK. Told you, I owe you. Still think those two in the Row Town saloon were minded to kill me whether I gave them the money or not. So reckon I wouldn't be here now if you hadn't shown up. So what do you need?'

As part of his escape plan, William had three requests. He wanted Alberto to get some food and water into the supply wagon. He also asked him to start a diversionary action at 2.45 a.m. and he needed to know whether the ex-miner, Hank, might have some dynamite stored somewhere.

'Yes. I know where it is,' confirmed Alberto, who seemed quite excited at the thought of being involved in the escape plan, especially when he was told the dreadful story of the treatment received by Carla and her murdered mother, Maria.

★　★　★

Around dusk, Rutherford and his two companions returned through the canyon.

Expecting some repercussions from the discovery that one of Rutherford's henchmen was missing, Sam and William were surprised that no hue and cry developed, though they feared for the kind of interrogation Carla might be receiving. As the darkness settled, William slipped out of the bunkhouse. Unseen, he worked his way to the rough pathway up the rocks to where he knew the interior canyon guard was stationed. It took him about forty minutes, including a break of ten minutes while he waited anxiously after he had disturbed a loose boulder and caused a noise, which might have alerted the guard.

When he reached the position where he knew the guard would be stationed he could see the man slumped against a rock in a posture which suggested slumber rather than alertness. He crept up behind the man and used his revolver to deliver a blow to the head, which would no doubt leave the victim nursing a bruise in the morning and wishing he had stayed fully awake. As he tied the man's hands and feet, William had only slight compassion for the tongue-lashing, or worse, which the man would no doubt have meted out to him the next morning.

The best part of another hour had passed before William had worked his way back to the floor of the canyon and then climbed up the other side to silence the other guard. This time it was easy to locate him, for the light of his cheroot glowed as a clear indication of his position.

This lookout was more alert, however, and turned when he sensed William approaching behind him. Startled, he grabbed for the Winchester on the ground beside him, giving William no choice but to act quickly and silence the man with a knife in his side. He then stabbed again to put the wounded sentry out of his agony.

Now less concerned about making a little noise, William quickly scrambled back down to the canyon floor and gathered up some of the dynamite sticks hidden away for him by Alberto.

With practised skill, he placed them strategically, with a long fuse running into the canyon. He then returned further into the main compound and placed further dynamite sticks under the Napoleon howitzer. Conscious that time was running out, he hurried back to the area where the wagon was kept and was relieved to find Sam and Carla already there.

Barely ten minutes later, they spotted the signal they were waiting for. In the heart of the hideout's main area Alberto had started a fire in a pile offence posts stacked against one of the buildings.

'That's it. Go now!' shouted William. Sam needed no second bidding. With Carla seated beside him, he started the wagon's four horses in a race towards the canyon entrance. Those already roused from their slumber to deal with the fire were slow to react to this new situation and the

107

wagon headed forward with not a single shot being fired towards them.

Alongside the wagon was William on his own horse, which he pulled to a halt when he reached the howitzer. He dismounted long enough to light the fuse, before riding on to his next objective, which was the much longer fuse leading into the canyon. As he lit that he was pleased to hear the explosion as the gun disintegrated behind him.

By now the wagon was well into the canyon and heading towards the exit, and William set out after it, hopeful that his second set of explosives would prevent any immediate pursuit by those in the hideout. Even he was surprised, however, by the thunderous roar which followed the ignition of the sticks he had placed in the rocky walls. It sounded as though half the mountain-side was crashing into the canyon and blocking the exit route for those inside the hideout.

There were now only two immediate

threats to their escape: the guards placed at the outer end of the canyon. William had acknowledged that there was no possible way he would have time to get to them in advance but he was gambling that they would be confused when they heard the explosions and would not know how to react.

Their job, after all, was to challenge anyone riding into the canyon, not those going in the opposite direction. They would also not be inclined to regard the wagon as a target, though it was clearly unusual for it to be leaving in the middle of the night.

In fact, William and the wagon were nearly out into the open before one of the guards belatedly decided something was wrong and fired off his Winchester at the escapees moving away from him. His shots had no impact and William did not even bother to return the fire as he pushed his mount to catch up with the wagon and help Sam pick up the moonlit trail leading them back in the direction of the border.

12

In fact, William's calculated timing had been very accurate. As night turned to day they were able to leave the trail and head into more broken land. He knew that the softer ground would make it easier for experienced trackers to follow the wagon's path, but he was counting on the blocked exit from the hideout giving them several hours' start.

If they could get across the river before the next nightfall, they would then have a reasonable chance of carefully setting a route on the other side, which would make tracking more difficult, and they could head for a town where they could seek the protection of the law.

William could have no idea, of course, what resources MacDonald might allocate to seeking reprisals. The Scot had only lost one wagon and that hardly warranted too much concern. And the loss of the girl was hardly a matter to worry MacDonald or anyone else except Rutherford, who would perhaps be forced to accept the possibility that his own missing gang member might be involved in the previous night's activities and that it was actually him that had somehow engineered the girl's escape. William considered that MacDonald might simply regard the whole business as being down to Rutherford to sort out for himself.

On the other hand, the episode was a major disruption to the hideout's normal smooth functioning and the lack of disturbance they had enjoyed for such a long time. MacDonald might take the view that the matter was a significant threat to their security and future operation, and therefore demand firm action. If nothing else, his hurt pride might, of itself, be enough to persuade him that he had to engineer punishment for those who had transgressed beyond the rules that he imposed on those who availed themselves of the facilities and security he provided.

On balance, therefore, William's experience of men like MacDonald left him in little doubt that, as soon as the canyon blockage was cleared, there would be hunters on their trail.

When they reached the Rio Grande, William and Sam were disturbed to find that the water level had risen since their previous crossing in the opposite direction. Although they had experienced no rain, there must have been a considerable fall up towards the river's faraway source in the Rocky Mountains.

William scouted in both directions and found what he considered to be the best point to ford the river but decided that it would be unwise to attempt a crossing in the gathering dusk.

Acknowledging how tired he was, William asked Sam to keep first watch after they had eaten so that he could grab some sleep himself.

At first light they started the crossing but found the task harder than they had expected. Two-thirds of the way across, the wagon lurched sideways and became lodged in the soft river bottom. No amount of urging the team would budge it and William cursed himself for the decision to escape with the wagon. His reasoning had been sound, in that he had reckoned the wagon would have been too useful to those in the hideout when they tried to clear the boulders piled up by the explosion. Without it, they would have had to construct Indian-style travois to haul the loose stuff away and clear a passage.

Now he had to consider whether he should cut the horses free from the wagon. First, however, they struggled in the flowing water to lighten the load as much as possible, and were surprised to find a false bottom to the interior of the wagon.

'That's twenty Winchesters that won't

finish up in the wrong hands,' grunted William as the discovered weapons were thrown overboard.

Suddenly a slight surge of water was enough to turn the wagon back to face the opposite bank they were aiming for and, with young Carla holding the reins and William and Sam hauling on ropes, the wagon suddenly moved forward again, and the weary and frightened horses seemed to find renewed strength as they somehow sensed that they could, after all, make it to safety.

By the time they had all reached the Texas bank the sun was already high in the sky and William and Sam agreed that, despite the possibility of pursuers, they should rest themselves and the animals during the burning heat of the day.

When they set off again, William adopted a system under which he scouted ahead to determine the best route and then doubled back behind the wagon to ensure that they weren't being followed. This meant that his mount was covering a considerable distance and when they reached more open country away from the river's bank, he had to abandon the backtracking as too demanding for the tired animal.

He could still not be certain in his mind what kind of force Ian MacDonald might deploy to seek retribution against those who had disturbed the equilibrium of his well-organized Mexican hideout. It was obvious, however, that they would stand no chance if pursuers caught up with them whilst they were still travelling back north, so he constantly urged his two tired young companions to push forward as quickly as possible.

What William could not have known, or even guessed, was that Alberto Lopez had already paid a horrible penalty for his involvement in the breakout that had given them their chance of freedom.

13

Awakened by the shouts coming from men already fighting the fire started by Alberto, Ian MacDonald had come out of the hacienda just as the dynamite set under the howitzer had exploded.

'What the hell is going on?' he demanded.

The Mexican henchman, Juan, started to reply, but then pointed to the surprising sight of the wagon already entering the mouth of the canyon, followed closely by William.

'Look, señor.' He pointed but didn't even bother to draw his revolver as he realized the shooting distance was too great for a hand weapon. 'It's that big fella on the horse.'

'Who was on the wagon?' asked MacDonald.

'Didn't see. But I guess it was that young nephew of his.'

'Well get mounted, quick. Grab a couple of others and get after them. Don't know what the hell they are up to, but I want them stopped. And why didn't the guards fire at them? Stupid fellas haven't got the intelligence of jackrabbits.'

He was talking to himself, however, as Juan had rushed to obey the earlier order. He and two others had hurried to get their horses and were soon headed towards the canyon in pursuit when the boom created by larger explosions echoed around the hideout.

MacDonald himself went to inspect the effect of the rockfall and quickly accepted that it was going to be many hours before anyone still inside the hideout would be able to exit through the blocked passageway.

He was busy organizing a working party when he was given more bad news. One of the bandits came to report that a dog had been pawing at soft ground where fencing work had been carried out. They had explored and found a body, which Rutherford had identified as his missing gang member.

'Rutherford also says the girl he brought in has gone missing,' reported the man to MacDonald, who was now seething with anger.

He demanded that Rutherford be brought to him and he was soon venting some of his anger at the bandit. 'What the hell is going on? Who killed your man? Was it that fella Ross that you were due to be taking with you tomorrow? And what's all this about the girl being missing? Who is she? I thought she was a relative of one of your lot.'

Rutherford was not sure how to answer, but decided the truth — or near truth — was the safest policy.

'No, she was an orphan we came across. We were sort of looking after her.'

MacDonald snorted. 'Yes, I can guess what sort of looking after she was getting from you lot! And what's her connection with this Ross, who seems to have caused us all this trouble?'

'We don't really know, Mr Mac-Donald, sir. Seems he might have come here with the idea of rescuing her. We guess he killed my man and has taken her in that wagon. As you know, I've been out of here with two of my men and we're honestly not sure how he's managed to arrange the escape.'

'Well Rutherford, you haven't heard the last of this. I'll be wanting you to get after him just as soon as we can get the entrance clear. I hold you to blame for what's gone on.'

As he dismissed Rutherford, Mac-Donald received the news that one of the two passageway guards had been killed and the other one had been found tied up and gagged.

'How on earth did Ross manage all that? He must have had help.'

Then, as he focussed his mind, he recalled that it had earlier been reported to him that Bert Lopez had been seen talking to the newcomers and had then had the opportunity of the trip into town to spend a great deal of time with the man who was obviously the cause of all that was going so wrong. He also realized that it was Lopez who had access to food and other supplies, as well as knowing where the dynamite was stored.

MacDonald was a man accustomed to getting others to do his dirty work for him, but when an apprehensive Alberto was dragged before him, the Scot's fury exploded as he personally grabbed a quirt and started thrashing at his victim.

It took less than ten minutes before Alberto, his clothes torn to shreds and his body covered in cuts from the vicious whip, lay dying in the dust after confessing his involvement with the escapees. His confession did him no good, however, for MacDonald hastened the man's end to life with a whole series of brutal kicks to his head and torso, bringing to fulfilment Alberto's own prediction that he would finish his days inside the hideout.

14

Despite constant fears that they would be tracked down, William, Sam and Carla continued their journey undisturbed.

At one point they lost their direction and turned north too early, away from the twisted course of the river. They found a homestead occupied by Joel and Raquel Holiday, a couple who had settled in Texas from Europe and now had two young children. With typical hospitality, they gave the travellers a hearty meal and pressed them to stay the night. At first William refused because he feared for their hosts if there were pursuers who could attack. He considered it was unfair to repay the family's hospitality by compromising their safety.

Carla, however, seemed to be so happy in the company of kind family folk after all her harsh treatment, that he had reluctantly agreed. He spent a restless night himself, though, and made sure they departed at first light the next day, armed with helpful directions to get them back to Carla's village. He offered payment before they left but the Holidays refused to accept anything, even though they were obviously struggling to make ends meet as they scratched a meagre existence from the land they cultivated.

William and Sam, together with Carla, continued through semi-desert until they reached the somewhat more hospitable area towards Plympton, where the mountains gradually gave way to more rounded hills interspersed with increasing amounts of grassland.

When they did arrive at the village they were soon overwhelmed. By now all the inhabitants knew the details of Maria's death and Carla's abduction and, within seconds of the wagon's arrival, they were surrounded by cheering folk delighted to welcome the young girl back.

Everyone wanted to reach up and shake hands and, although it was not one of the customary times of day, the church bells were soon added to the general cacophony. In fact Carla eventually had to plead with the delighted neighbours to let them cover the last little stretch to her father's cantina.

As they approached, they could see her brother and father outside, checking why the bells should be pealing at this time of day and concerned that something might be wrong. From a distance, Carla yelled excitedly. 'Pa, Anton! It's me. I'm back.'

Immediately, they began running towards the wagon with such haste that Sam had to bring the team to a rapid halt before father and son were trampled underfoot.

Carla jumped down and embraced her relatives, with tears streaming down all their faces. Sam and William watched the scene of unconfined joy with an almost equal feeling of pleasure at the reunion, before they, too, were pulled into the embraces. 'Thank you. Thank you,' said Hawkins repeatedly as he grasped their hands and pulled them both into bear hugs. 'How did you find her?'

'We'll tell you later, but for now we need to see to the horses,' said William, trying to bring a little sanity back into the occasion. 'And some food for us would be much appreciated.'

After they had eaten a satisfying meal of beef stew, William took Hawkins aside. Without revealing anything further about the deprivations and degradations his daughter might have suffered, he explained his fears that reprisals would be sought for the havoc they had caused in the Mexican hideout.

'I don't want to worry you overmuch, friend, but I fear that they will come lookin' for us and possibly want to recapture Carla. They know this place from stayin' here before, and will guess that we've brought her back home. Is there somewhere you can go, rather than stay here?'

Their host's face clouded over at the thought of reprisals, but he confirmed that he was sure they could stay with the town's schoolteacher, a man called Oliver. 'He's a good friend. He runs a small school and teaches the local children. Carla and Anton have both been taught by him. He effectively runs a charity, with the townsfolk repaying him with whatever they can afford. His wife is a lovely woman called Rebecca. She comes from a German family and I'm sure she would let us stay with them if you think it would be safer. But what about you and Sam? What will you do?'

'With your permission, we'll stay here in your cantina. If I'm right, we're gonna be targets whether we stay or go. So I figure we might as well stay where they can find us, and get the thing over.'

'But that's crazy. You can't know how many they'll send. You won't stand a chance.'

'Let me worry about that, my friend. But there's something you can do for us. Can you get someone from the town to ride to the sheriff and tell him what's happened? Lazy as he is, the sheriff can hardly fail to come to our aid if we deliver the rogues right into his jurisdiction.'

After this was arranged, William and Sam prepared to fortify the cantina as best they could. In practice, this defensive action consisted of little more than using furniture to block doors and deciding where the two of them would place themselves to get the best views of attackers.

Sam did not attempt to cover up his fears that they would be overwhelmed if MacDonald sent a major force against them.

'I don't think that's likely,' his uncle assured him. 'Remember that the men in the hideout aren't actually obliged to follow his orders. My guess is that they won't see chasing us down as a priority. They are greedy men and there's nothing in it for them. Most of them will see it more as a problem for Rutherford than for themselves. As there are only two of us, I'll be very surprised if more than five or six come out to find us, and we should be able to cope with that — even if they arrive before the sheriff joins us with his deputies.'

'I sure hope you're right,' his nephew sighed. He was still not convinced that his uncle's confidence was well placed, but he was determined not to show how scared he was at the prospect of being attacked.

15

The blockage to the canyon must have been even more difficult to clear than William had calculated, because another two days elapsed before the reprisals team arrived.

There were seven of them. Rutherford and his two surviving henchmen; Hank, the man in black; MacDonald's Mexican gunman, Juan; one of the Indians, who had probably acted as their tracker; and one other man they had seen at the hideout but didn't know.

They announced their arrival with a single shot into the air.

'You in there, Grant?' challenged Rutherford. 'Yep, we know who you are. It was the last thing Lopez told us before he died.'

'I'm here,' replied William. 'You killed Lopez?'

'Nope, not me. MacDonald did it himself. Now who you got with you?'

William declined to answer the question. Instead he posed his own. 'What do you want, Rutherford?'

'You, for a start, Grant. Dead or alive, but preferably dead. And we want our girl back that you stole.'

There was anger and disbelief combined in William's reply. 'What do you mean? After all you've done to her, you dare to call her your girl? She's back with her father, safe from further assault by you beasts.'

As he looked out, William saw the Mexican, Juan, turn to Rutherford at his side. He could not hear their exchange but it looked like a heated argument. Perhaps it was the first time Juan realized that the girl had been captured and taken to the hideout against her will, to be used as a plaything.

The two men continued their war of words for some while before Juan spat on the ground, wheeled his horse round and started off away from the cantina. Without comment, the Yaqui Indian also turned his horse and joined the Mexican. They didn't get far, though — only a few yards — before two shots rang out. Both men were killed by neat bullet holes in their backs. The bandit, Rutherford, returned his revolver to its holster.

★   ★   ★

Watching the scene from inside the cantina Sam and William were surprised at Rutherford's hasty action, but could only feel relief that the odds against them had narrowed. Now it was just five against two; they didn't have to wait long before the confrontation got underway.

Rutherford and his two men urged their horses round the side of the building whilst the other unknown bandit and the man in black took up positions behind two stacks of wood and other building materials.

With William at the front of the building and Sam protecting the rear, a position of stalemate developed with only sporadic exchanges of fire having no effect other than to remind each side that the other was still there.

Inside the building Sam called out to his companion. 'So what we gonna do? It will get dark soon and we won't be able to see them if they decide to come closer.'

'We've got to sit it out, son. I was hoping that the sheriff and his deputy might show up, but I don't think we can rely on them gettin' here any time soon.'

As he spoke, however, there was a crash from the unprotected side of the building. Unseen by Sam, Rutherford and his two companions had used a fence pole to force their way through a side door. Unsure exactly where Sam was located, two of them came in shooting wildly but there was still sufficient light behind them for Sam to identify their shapes. As he fired he felt searing pain from his upper leg, where a randomly fired bullet had successfully found a target. But his own shots had been even more successful; two attackers had been felled and no movement came from either of them slumped on the floor.

'You OK?' yelled William, and was only partly reassured when his young companion confirmed that he was still alive but couldn't move.

Then William was shouted at by Hank, the man in black. 'I've waited long enough, Grant. Your time is up.'

As he spoke, William spotted that the man with Hank was approaching with a lighted bundle of straw tied to a pole. They were obviously going to use the old trick of setting fire to the building and smoking their opponents out into the open.

In their impatience, however, they had made a basic miscalculation. As the man with the flare approached in the half-light of dusk, he was lit up as an easy target. It was childishly simple for

William to line him up and fire two shots, which brought the man to the ground in an untidy heap, with no movement coming from the lifeless body lit up by the dying flare.

'Like easy targets, do you?' taunted the man in black. 'Why don't you come out and face me like a man? See how easy that is! Fancy a fair fight?'

William found himself faced with a difficult decision. He could not know how badly injured Sam was behind him or whether Rutherford and his men were alive or dead. If he let the stalemate continue indefinitely it was possible that the young man could bleed to death, or again be attacked from the side or rear of the building.

On the other hand, the man in black was obviously a skilled shootist, who considered himself at least equal to any opponent in a straight firearms duel. It was possibly too much of a risk to accept the challenge from a man who had come to the West as a miner but had been seduced by the romanticism of storytellers spreading truths, and myths, about characters like Wild Bill Hickok.

Again, though, the man issued his taunting challenge. 'Come on, Grant. What you waitin' for? Just you and me. I'm prepared to show myself in the open if you'll be man enough to come and face up to me.'

William was still undecided, until Sam called out. 'What's happenin'? I'm pretty sure I got two who came in here, but I can't stop my leg from bleeding.'

That was enough to make up William's mind. It might be suicidal, but he decided that he had to act. He reloaded and replied to his challenger.

'OK. Come out into the open and I'll come out and meet you,' he yelled.

'No tricks, Grant?'

'No tricks. Fair fight, Hank. Just you and me.'

And that's how it worked out. Both men came out into the open and walked to face each other squarely in the gloom of dusk. Feet planted firmly apart in the standard stance of the gunman, they stood in silence for several minutes before the man in black called out in a controlled voice: 'OK, Grant. Make your move.'

In response William made a sideways movement of his head. It was enough to trigger a response from his opponent, who drew and fired, once only, with lightning speed. To Hank's surprise, however, he found that he had missed his target. Instead of going straight for his own holster, William had dived to the ground, drawing only as he rolled to his side and then firing up at the man who had been sure he had the quickest draw.

At first the man in black stood firm as, in quick succession, three bullets cut into his body. But then he slumped forward, first on to his knees and then slowly further forward until he was flat on the ground. As he did so in slow motion, William was sure he could see a smile on the man's face. Perhaps he had died in the way he desired when he first donned his ostentatious black outfit.

As William walked towards the dead man he admitted to himself that he had a grudging admiration for the way the man had made a decision to re-shape his life, and then his death, in a setting far removed from his mining-town upbringing miles across the Atlantic.

It was a better death, William considered, than that suffered by the thousands who had come to the end of their lives on the bloody battlefields of the Civil War or, even worse, died slowly from horrendous injuries in grubby, ill-equipped field hospitals.

As he looked down at the Englishman he could not help, just for a moment, considering his own mortality and wondering whether he, too, would die with dignity.

His thoughts were soon interrupted, though, by the sound of a horse heading away from the scene of the day's battle and by his deep concern for his nephew.

16

Although Sam's arterial injury was serious, professional treatment by the town's sawbones saved his leg — and his life.

Hawkins, Carla and her brother resumed life in the cantina and the girl, though mentally scarred, seemed ready to accept that she still had a future worth facing after her terrible ordeal.

Sheriff Goodrich and his deputy had shown up the day after the shooting. The sheriff was able to identify the man who had approached with the flare intended to burn down the Hawkins' cantina. Apparently he had carried out a bank robbery two years earlier. Although he had not been seen since he escaped with the proceeds, the bank still had a $500 reward out for him.

Because of what the bandits had done to Maria and Carla, the two men with Rutherford also had small bounty rewards placed on them. Both had been killed by Sam, who insisted that the reward money should be given to Carla.

Somewhat surprisingly, the man in black had no record of previous wrongdoings and nothing was known either about the Mexican, Juan or the Indian who had died with him when they turned away from the cantina after learning that Carla had been ill-treated and abducted.

Of the cantina's seven attackers, only one was left to be accounted for. There was no sign of Rutherford at the scene of the shootings and it was obvious that it had been the gang leader William had heard riding away when he had realized that he was on the losing side.

When pressed by William, the sheriff confirmed that there was still a substantial reward for Rutherford's capture or death. Sam and the Hawkins family were dismayed, however, when William declared his intention to chase after him.

'We've still got unfinished business,' he said. 'Rutherford was in charge when Maria was murdered and Carla was raped and he came chasing after us when we got out of the hideout. No doubt he would not have hesitated to kill all of us if he had the chance, especially if he was acting on Mac-Donald's orders. I'm gonna bring him in.'

Seeing William's determination, the sheriff said he would get up a posse but was taken aback when William vehemently resisted the suggestion.

'It's only one man and I honestly think I'll stand a better chance of apprehending him if I go alone. I can travel quicker by myself and he's less likely to be aware of being tracked by one hunter than if there's a whole posse on his trail.'

The sheriff argued that it was up to the law to act, rather than have William act alone, but accepted that there was nothing he could do to stop him setting out before a posse could be formed. He eventually agreed. 'OK. It's up to you. But if you're successful I insist that you bring him back here and hand him over to me. What's more, I want you wearing a deputy's badge, so it's all legal.'

So when William Grant rode out two days after the shooting, he was back to wearing a lawman's badge on his vest. He went alone, having turned down Sam's proposal that he come along too. 'I thought we were supposed to be a team, working together,' Sam had argued, but William would have none of it.

'Sure, we've worked well together,' he acknowledged, 'but this really is a one-man job. Besides anything else, that injured leg of yours is gonna take some time to heal properly, and it's best that I set off soon before the trail goes completely cold.'

In practice, though, there was not much tracking involved. Once William had established that Rutherford had set off towards the south, he decided to take a gamble that the outlaw was heading again to the safety of Mac-Donald's hideout. He calculated that his best chance of catching Rutherford was to get ahead of him and lay a trap, rather than keep chasing behind and thereby making himself vulnerable to an ambush. There was no way he wanted to expose himself to the strong possibility of being bushwhacked by an opponent who, unlike the man in black, would have no concept of a fair fight.

Surprisingly, given his opposition to what he regarded as 'damn bounty hunting', the sheriff had excelled himself by providing a fresh mount — a strong sorrel with a stride that gobbled up the miles. William rode on with a minimum of rests in a determined effort to get across the border before his quarry. He had no idea where Rutherford would attempt to cross into Mexico but the lawman decided that his best chance of success would be to push on and intercept the bandit on the well-trodden trail nearer the hideout, which the outlaw was almost bound to use for the last few miles, hopefully whilst looking over his shoulder rather than expecting an attack from ahead. He was determined to take Rutherford back alive if at all possible, but was prepared to accept that a shootout might well have to be the outcome if he successfully confronted the bandit before he got back to MacDonald's safe haven.

Despite his badge, William knew that he had no authority on the Mexican side of the border, but he decided that was of no real significance. The important thing was to get the job done, without worrying too much about the legalities. He hadn't gone far into the pursuit before he removed the badge from his vest and tucked it inside his clothing. If he met anyone else on his journey, he wanted to remain anonymous so that he was not delayed by getting involved in anything other than the chase.

★　★　★

On his sturdy mount he made excellent progress; he had no difficulty fording the river and pushed on until he calculated that he was no more than ten miles away from the entrance to the canyon which formed the passageway to MacDonald's sanctuary. He picked a spot where he could safely leave his mount grazing on a hidden area of sparse grass. Before he left it, however, he carefully removed Rutherford's poster from his saddle-bag, added some food and a canteen of water and then backtracked to where he planned to climb a low rocky cliff which looked down on the trail. Prior to hiding himself away, however, he stopped at a wizened tree right beside the narrow trail he was trusting Rutherford would use. He spiked the poster on to a protruding broken branch where he knew that anyone approaching could not fail to see it.

He then climbed to his chosen lookout point and prepared for a long wait as the sun sank behind the mountains and the sky darkened. Confident that Rutherford would not ride the difficult trail throughout the night, William satisfied his hunger with some dried food and allowed himself to drift into a shallow sleep despite the lizards scuttling around him on the ledge.

Early in the morning he was alerted by a small flock of birds taking off noisily. He guessed that they had been disturbed by some sort of predator or an approaching rider. A few minutes later he had the satisfaction of seeing a single horseman approaching steadily along the trail. If it was Rutherford then he could congratulate himself on his dual strategy of getting ahead of him and correctly positioning himself at a spot that his quarry would pass on his way to the safety of the hideout.

With his Winchester at the ready, William waited patiently until the rider reached the tree with the poster attached. At that distance he was able to confirm that the horseman was indeed the man he had earlier seen when the revenge party had arrived at the Hawkins' cantina. As he expected, Rutherford saw the poster and pulled his mount to a halt so that he could examine it in detail.

William could imagine the man's amazement at seeing his own image so unexpectedly staring at him in this remote spot, and his bewilderment at how it might have got there. He watched as Rutherford ripped the poster from the tree and stuffed it into his clothing.

'Yep. It's you all right,' shouted William. 'And I've got you covered. So drop your weapons before I put a bullet in you.'

At this, Rutherford turned his horse and dismounted over the flank opposite William's vantage point. Stood behind the animal, he pulled his own rifle from its scabbard and rested it over the saddle. 'Who's that?' he called.

'William Grant,' came the reply. 'And I'm aiming to take you back. Dead or alive. So why don't you act sensible and give yourself up.'

'No way, Grant. What's the point in goin' back with you when I know I'll finish up hangin' from a rope?' As he spoke, the outlaw reinforced his words by firing up at the cliff side. His aim was way off target, indicating that he could not see William or pinpoint his position from the sound of his voice. His action was a clear signal, however, that he had no intention of simply giving himself up without a fight.

Despite his previous manhunting experience, William wasn't sure how best to react to his opponent's defiance. Hidden behind his horse, Rutherford did not present a clear target. In any case, the ex-marshal maintained his desire to take the man back alive if possible. Despite Rutherford's law-breaking record, William preferred to let a court decide the man's fate, rather than use his own rifle as judge, jury and executioner.

'Your last chance, Rutherford,' he

shouted in order to test the man's resolve. 'Throw your weapons aside or I'll shoot to kill.'

The response was another hopeful shot from down below. This time it was a little closer to its target. William decided that he had to add a bullet to his words. Taking account of his own height on the ledge, he aimed carefully at a spot a few feet before the horse below him, hoping that he could disturb the animal and leave its owner more exposed. His tactic did not work out as he had hoped, however, because his bullet ricocheted off the rocky ground and shot up into the animal's flank just in front of the saddle. From his distant position, he could not see exactly what had happened but the stricken animal reared up with an almost-human scream and jerked itself away from Rutherford's grasp. It took three or four steps forward and reared up again, before sinking slowly to its knees with a horrible moaning sound.

Left exposed, Rutherford called up.

'The poor beast is in agony, Grant. Hold your fire and let me put it out of its misery.' As he spoke, he moved towards the injured horse, put his rifle to its head and fired twice to put an end to its life. But Rutherford's act was not simply one of compassion for an animal that had served him well. He immediately dropped down behind the collapsed beast so that he could use its body as a shield. Once again he fired up at his unseen target.

'What you gonna do now, Grant? You can't come down and get me. I'll get you first as soon as you show yourself.'

'No hurry,' came the reply. 'I reckon I'm a sight more comfortable up here than you are squattin' behind that horse. Won't be long before you cramp up. I'm happy to wait until you've had enough and decide to give yourself up.'

17

As time passed, William began to wonder if his tactics were wrong. Down below him, Rutherford seemed content to stay where he was behind his dead horse. Perhaps he had been shrewd enough to realize that, as the sun passed its zenith, it would be shining straight into William's eyes and his positional advantage would be effectively negated.

The stalemate continued for a considerable time before William was caught off guard by a sudden movement from the man below. Instead of backing away from the direction of his opponent, Rutherford raced across the narrow trail and quickly got to the foot of William's cliff in a position where he could not be seen from the overhanging perch above.

'So what happens now, Grant?' he

shouted. 'You can't see me and I can't see you, but you can't stay up there for ever and I can slip away as soon as it gets dark. I just heard your horse whinnying, so I know what direction it's in and I reckon from down here I can reach it before you can. All I gotta do then is ride to MacDonald's place and bring some men out to hunt you down. You ain't gonna get far on foot.'

William did not reply. Although he didn't like to admit it to himself, he reluctantly acknowledged that logic was on Rutherford's side. He knew that if he stayed where he was, the chances were that the man below would indeed get to the horse before he could get along the ridge and down to ground level himself. Deliberately staying silent so that Rutherford couldn't get a fix on his position, the experienced man-hunter was forced to recognize that he had miscalculated. He was unsure how to proceed. For the moment, at least, he was outmanoeuvred.

Again Rutherford called out. 'So you

gonna come down?'

Again William chose not to reply and the silence continued as both men considered their next move. It stayed that way until well past noon, but unexpectedly it was an outside intervention that broke the deadlock. At first neither of the men could place the sound that gently echoed off the rock face. As they strained their ears the mystery was solved when an old Mexican goatherd appeared round a twist in the trail with a handful of scrawny animals being encouraged along by his prodding with a broken branch. Much more importantly as far as Rutherford was concerned was the fact that the old man was also leading a mule.

The Mexican stopped in his tracks when he spotted Rutherford and his dead horse on opposite sides of the trail. His natural assumption would have been that the horse had stumbled and broken a leg so that it had to be put down by his rider. The dilemma for the

Mexican, though, was that he was now faced by an armed gringo who would probably have no compunction about shooting him and stealing the mule. Knowing there was no escape, the poor man raised his hands in the air and continued slowly in Rutherford's direction.

From his vantage point William could see the Mexican and his animals, but could still not get a sight of Rutherford. This changed, however, when the bandit hurried across to the goatherd with his hands spread out in a gesture designed to indicate that he meant no harm. What he achieved was the advantage of being able to place himself beside the Mexican and the mule in a position he calculated would deter William from firing for fear of hitting the innocent goatherd. Though the bandit would not have hesitated to kill the old man himself, he guessed that his opponent on the cliff above him would not be so callous.

His calculation was correct and

William could only watch passively as the wanted man walked away from him, gesticulating and chatting to the Mexican as if he were an old friend and even using his own rifle to help prod the man's animals along the trail.

As soon as they had slowly progressed out of range, the frustrated lawman started the difficult scramble down the cliff side, roundly cursing himself for having been so comprehensively outfoxed by his quarry, but determined to make amends in the next stage of their cat and mouse game. Not particularly athletic, and still hampered by an old leg wound inflicted in an earlier shootout, William struggled to follow the two men ahead of him. Despite the relatively short distance to be covered, he was soon sweating profusely in the heat of the remaining afternoon sun.

After a while, however, he could hear Rutherford shouting at the Mexican in a garbled mixture of English and as many Spanish words as the bandit could muster. Their position was just past where he had left the horse he had borrowed from the sheriff. William guessed that Rutherford was annoyed that he had not immediately found it and was ordering the Mexican to help him locate the animal, which had been left hobbled in a small grassy area quite well hidden in the rocky edge of the mountain range which rose up from the trail.

Relieved that Lady Luck now seemed to be favouring him rather than Rutherford, William continued on foot past his hidden horse towards the raised voices, but was concerned to hear a further shot from what had to be Rutherford's rifle.

William could easily discover where the two men were because a couple of the goats were still on the trail and he could hear voices coming from around a projecting area of the rock face. At least the voices indicated that Rutherford had not killed the old man, as William had feared. When he rounded the rock he found that he was only a few feet away from a strange scene in which the old Mexican was on his knees, splattered with blood which had obviously come from the goat he was holding in his arms like a baby. Rutherford, with his back to William, was looking down on the Mexican with his rifle held loosely by his side.

'This time you really had better drop that weapon,' warned William, 'or else there's no second chance. Don't like doin' it but I've been forced to shoot men in the back before, so don't think I'll fight shy of doin' it again if you don't do what I say.'

Rutherford turned his head, without making any attempt to drop the rifle.

'I mean it. Drop it now — or else,' William ordered, and this time Rutherford obeyed, as he saw the Winchester pointed at him. 'OK, Grant,' he responded, bending his knees to lower his rifle. He stayed in that position for a fraction too long, however, and an alert William immediately suspected that his opponent was going to go for his holstered handgun as soon as the rifle was on the ground. 'Stop or you're dead!' he shouted.

The urgent warning was enough to remove any foolhardy thoughts from Rutherford's mind. Slowly standing upright, he then raised his hands to shoulder height and unexpectedly grinned in recognition that he had lost this round in their ongoing battle of wits.

'Now that's being sensible,' commented William. 'I meant it, you know. Don't really matter to me whether I take you back alive or dead, though I'd rather like to give young Carla a chance to see you get your just deserts. Now — slowly, slowly — get rid of the gunbelt then take three steps away from me.'

Still without speaking, Rutherford obeyed and William turned his attention to the goatherd. The man was still squatting on the ground with the dead animal cradled in his arms. No doubt he would already have formed a loathing towards the American who had initially seemed friendly but, in reality, had only wanted a shield and had then shot the precious goat. But there was no way the Mexican could be certain that the new *gringo* now holding a rifle was any less of a danger than the first one.

Recognizing this, William reached inside his clothing and found the deputy's badge presented to him by Sheriff Goodrich. In sign language he indicated that he was the legitimate owner of a lawman's right to capture a lawbreaker. The Mexican smiled an acknowledgement of this and then turned to shake an angry fist at the man who had shot his goat.

With his rifle constantly trained on Rutherford, William used a combination of sign language, English and Spanish to get the goatherd to tie Rutherford's hands behind him and retrieve the man's discarded rifle and handgun. Then there followed a protracted negotiation which eventually resulted in agreement that the Mexican would exchange the mule and the dead goat for Rutherford's weapons, gunbelt and ammunition.

Watching this drawn out procedure, Rutherford suddenly interjected: 'Why the hell don't you just shoot the bastard instead of arguing all day?'

'Because my name ain't Rutherford and I don't reason like you. Now let's see how easily you can get up on that mule with your hands tied.'

'What! You expect me to ride that critter?'

'You can walk if you prefer, but it's a pretty long way. So why don't we just get on with it? And, by the way, you'll be taking the goat with you,' added William with relish as he watched Rutherford's look of utter disgust.

When they left the goatherd and returned to the outlaw's dead horse to remove some of the contents of the saddle-bags, Rutherford demanded to know what was going to happen to his expensive saddle.

'Ain't gonna be much use to you in future,' commented William. 'The old man will no doubt return for it later when he realizes it's there for the taking. I reckon he's gonna end up feelin' pretty pleased he ran into you today, despite the scare and trouble you gave him.'

'Should have given him more trouble than that,' grunted Rutherford. 'And you, too, with your Wanted poster stoppin' me the way you did.'

William remembered that Rutherford had kept the poster. 'Think I'll have your picture back,' he demanded. 'Worth keepin' safe, I reckon.'

18

As they started on their return journey, Rutherford complained constantly about his sore backside and how difficult it was to stay seated upright with his hands tied behind him, even though his captor was guiding the mule with a rough halter.

'Rutherford, why don't you quit moanin' and save your breath? You can talk when we make camp tonight. There's a few things I want to know.'

In fact, Rutherford was quite garrulous when they settled down after eating that evening. Not at all wary of admitting his guilty past, he actually seemed anxious to impress William with details of a long list of crimes carried out with his small gang. Robbery, arson, horse theft and murder were included in his list of misdeeds.

'And what about raping a young

girl?' demanded his listener, who had mentally logged the man's boastful claims as information he could pass on to the authorities, who would almost certainly condemn Rutherford to the gallows.

'Rape? No, I never done that. Never needed to.'

'But you let your pardners do it, without attempting to stop them.'

'Yep. But you gotta let the fellas have a bit of leeway, to keep 'em loyal,' conceded Rutherford, without any trace of regret in his voice. 'It ain't easy to keep 'em in line if you don't let 'em live a bit.'

'My heart bleeds for you,' sneered William. 'Must be real hard being leader of a bunch of crooks. Now tell me what happened to poor Lopez back at MacDonald's place.'

In graphic detail, Rutherford described the savage whipping Alberto Lopez had endured before his torn body could take no more. 'He told us about you before he died, though. How your name wasn't really Ross and that you had been a damn bounty hunter when he met up with you before. He also admitted that he helped with your escape from Glencoe. Confession didn't do him any good, though. Just made MacDonald even madder as he laid it on with the whip. Never seen a man so cut up. Surprised he lasted as long as he did. For a little fella, he had a lot of endurance.'

'Didn't anyone stop MacDonald?'

'Nope. Don't think they all liked to see it. Old Bert was harmless, and it was brutal, but no one wanted to cross MacDonald. Gettin' on the wrong side of that wild Scot ain't a good idea . . . '

Disgusted at what he heard, William resolved that, if he were ever to meet up with Alberto's killer again, he would ensure that the man would be fully repaid in kind for his actions.

In fact Rutherford's information planted in William's mind the seed of an idea that MacDonald should somehow be brought to justice, even though at this stage the only charges that could be brought against him would be giving refuge to criminals in a foreign country, and that procedure involved a degree of legal nicety that was beyond William's knowledge of the law.

Either as a lawman, or a bounty hunter, he had always seen his job as tracking down wrongdoers and handing them over to the authorities, rather than deciding what punishment should be meted out to them.

★   ★   ★

In his determination and haste to set out after Rutherford, William had neglected to bring any proper handcuffs with him. Now, in addition to leaving the bandit's hands tied at the wrists, he put further binding round his captive's feet at night.

The next morning, Rutherford complained bitterly about the discomfort he had suffered.

'How about me swearin' I won't try to escape if you ease up on the rope?'

Rutherford pleaded.

'No chance! I wouldn't take your word if you held a Bible in your hand and swore over your mother's grave.'

Surprisingly, Rutherford laughed. 'I'd have trouble doin' that,' he said. 'Bible don't mean nothin' to me and I don't even know whether the old hag is dead or alive. I left her when I was ten years old and ain't been in touch with any family since I took our only horse and rode off.'

As William reached over to untie Rutherford's feet, his captive seemed relaxed and ready to accept that his upper body movement would continue to be restrained as he rode the mule. But as the binding round his ankles was released he suddenly bent his knees and then thrust both feet at Williams's chest, throwing him on to his back.

Despite the cramping his legs must have suffered from his restricted movement during the night, Rutherford managed to get to his feet first. He kicked William in the thigh but, with his hands still tied, was off balance as he prepared to lash out again. Desperately, William launched himself at the bandit from his kneeling position. The two men crashed to the ground together, but this time it was William who managed to roll away and get to his feet first.

He drew his .45 and pointed it at Rutherford as the man struggled to his knees.

'OK', he warned. 'That's it. I told you before that I don't care if I take you back alive or dead. Any more tricks like that and it'll sure be dead. This is your last warning. Now let's get movin'. We've got a lot of ground to cover.'

★ ★ ★

With a mixture of riding and walking they made good progress, despite the slow speed of the mule. They were approaching the river when Rutherford drew attention to rising dust in the distance. It seemed to be coming in their direction and the two men concluded that it was caused by at least four riders.

'Better hide up, I reckon,' said William, and headed for a small copse of trees off the rough trail they had been following.

'Look like *rurales*, with their uniforms,' said Rutherford. 'Come across 'em before. Always wondered how MacDonald managed to keep 'em away from us. Even though they are supposed to be an official rural police force, they seem to pretty much please themselves. I've been told a lot of 'em are released jailbirds themselves and they ain't against dishing out their own kinda justice. It's said they don't take prisoners. Most ordinary Mexicans hate them like poison.'

As they waited for the small group to pass on the lower ground in front of them, William kept his Colt aimed at Rutherford. Despite the man's spoken mistrust of the Mexicans, it was possible that he might take the chance of drawing their attention and throwing his lot in with them rather than facing the near-certainty of jail or a hanging when he was handed back to the authorities once they were back over the border. Under the threat of a bullet from William's Colt, however, he remained silent, and the danger passed.

It seemed to William that his captive was now more resigned to his fate. As the bindings gradually cut more into his wrists, Rutherford carried on moaning about that and the discomfort of riding what he constantly described as 'that damn mule', but he made no further attempts to frustrate William's determination to get him back to civilization — and justice.

In fact the only incident that marked their journey back into Southern Texas was when the rough trail they were following took them down a steep incline of reddish shale.

Both men dismounted as their animals struggled to keep upright on the slippery surface, with the mule making better progress than William's larger animal. Keeping up with his mule, Rutherford reached the bottom of the slope first as William scrambled down with his heavier sorrel.

At the foot of the slope, Rutherford shouted up to William. 'What you waitin' for, buddy? Thought you were supposed to be leadin' the way! For a moment there I thought I might leave you and carry on by myself. You sure you don't wanna swap animals? Perhaps you'd like to get a sore backside like me?'

As he reached the bottom of the incline, William acknowledged the ironic touch of sick humour in his captive's comments. Strangely, a sort of rapport, or at least understanding, seemed to be developing as Rutherford apparently accepted that his future life was now firmly under William's control.

Nevertheless, the man who had now pinned his badge back on to his vest remained wary. He wasn't prepared to relax his caution until he had safely handed Rutherford over to face justice. Given the bandit's many admitted transgressions, there was no way of knowing what skulduggery he might be capable of committing.

The need for caution and continued mistrust was firmly demonstrated during the following night. Desperately tired from the journey and the effort of having to keep a constant eye on his captive, William could not stop himself falling into a deeper sleep.

As usual, he had bound Rutherford's feet and tied him to the saddle removed from his own horse, so that the man would have difficulty moving from where he was bedded down several feet away.

But using a sharply edged rock Rutherford worked for a couple of hours to saw through the bindings behind his back. Despite the fact that he had badly cut his hands in the process of untying himself, he was able to get free from the saddle and stumble over to where the lawman was in what still seemed to be a fairly sound sleep. He bent down to grasp the Winchester, which William had tucked under his bedroll. He was just removing it when his captor came out of his slumber and immediately realized the danger he was in. He looked up and saw Rutherford crouched above him with the weapon grasped in his bloodied hands.

Rutherford swung wildly and was about to bring the butt down on to him when, just in time, William managed to roll away. He missed William's head by inches and cursed loudly as the weapon jarred against the ground and sent a painful shock through his body, causing him to lose his grip on the rifle, and grasp his elbow in agony.

He saw his opponent start to scramble to his feet, but launched himself before the lawman could get upright. The two men crashed to the ground together and were soon embraced in a mutual bear hug, giving advantage to neither of them as they struggled in the dusty surface. They rolled together as each man tried to adjust his own grip or position, whilst seeking to stop the other from gaining a superior hold.

At one point Rutherford managed to push his knee up into William's groin but without sufficient force to make his opponent loosen his grip.

In fact William managed to twist his body and was surprised when the other man broke his hold and rolled away. There was a sickening crunch, however, as Rutherford's head hit a rock and his whole body went limp.

William quickly got to his feet and was relieved to realize that Rutherford was not moving.

Wary of being tricked, he retrieved his Colt and held it to Rutherford's head as he felt for a pulse. He was able to ascertain that the bandit was unconscious rather than dead and quickly acted to tie him again before he regained his senses.

For the second time on their journey, Rutherford had demonstrated his cunning in appearing to accept his fate, but had then created an opportunity to attack his captor in a bid to escape. But it had done him no good. When he came round, he once again found himself bound and captive.

19

After Rutherford's second attempted attack, the rest of the journey up into Texas passed without further problems.

William deliberately followed the return route he had taken earlier with Sam and Carla, knowing it would bring him to the Holidays' homestead he had visited before. He was concerned that they might resent his further intrusion into their privacy and hospitality, but the reverse was true. Joel and Raquel Holiday welcomed him with genuine delight and were excited and impressed when he explained that his captive was the leader of the gang which had abducted Carla.

'Are you really a badman?' their daughter Anna boldly asked Rutherford.

He hesitated before replying, as if giving careful consideration to a straight and fair question. Eventually, he looked the little girl in the eye, and crouched down to her level, causing her to back away a few steps as she listened to his reply. 'Guess your ma and pa would think so,' he conceded. 'But sometimes things just don't work out the way good folk might expect and some of us take the wrong path on life's journey. I weren't like you, little one, 'cause I didn't have a ma and pa to love me properly, so I left them and then started to do bad things, which I guess I'll have to pay for when I go before the judge.'

'Will they lock you up for what you've done?'

'That's probably the best I can hope for, young lady,' Rutherford replied, involuntarily reaching up to touch his neck as he acknowledged what the future possibly held for him.

Anxious to stop Anna's questions going any deeper, her mother hustled the youngster off to bed.

'What happens now?' Joel asked William.

'Well, I hesitate to ask this when you were so kind to us before but I would like us to sleep in your barn tonight. And can you tell me where's the nearest lawman to here, Mr Holiday? I don't want to rely on the sheriff, who wasn't exactly in favour of me trying to capture Rutherford by myself. I think he'll be more than a bit upset to learn that I've succeeded without his help.' As an afterthought, however, he did acknowledge that he was riding the sheriff's horse. 'Suppose I at least owe him for that.'

'Well there's a town marshal in Littleford,' Holiday told him. 'It is only twelve miles away. His name is Matt Normington. Will you be takin' Rutherford there in the morning? Normington is a good man who is well respected by us all, and he's got a secure jail for your villain.'

'That sounds perfect,' said William, 'but I'm afraid I've got another favour to ask. Would it be possible for you to ride in with me? Rutherford has been a might tricky and I'd hate to lose him at this stage of the game.'

'Sure I can manage that, though I'm surprised you feel you need any help after all you've done. But right now I can smell cookin' so let's get to make sure this fella's well secured and then you can tell me and Raquel the whole story of what happened after you got Carla home.'

⋆ ⋆ ⋆

The next morning William sat and wrote a note and wrapped it in a small parcel along with the badge given to him by Sheriff Goodrich in Sheerwater. 'It's my formal resignation as a deputy,' he explained to Joel. 'You and me are goin' to deliver Rutherford as private citizens.'

When the trio arrived at Marshal Normington's office the next morning, William showed the law officer Rutherford's Wanted poster, and handed him the deputy's badge and the letter he had written at the homestead.

'We're handin' this wanted man over to you, Marshal, and Holiday and me are claiming the reward it shows on the poster. Please make sure Mr Holiday here gets it, and I'll come and get my share off him later.'

At first the homesteader was speechless, but when they went outside the marshal's office he tackled William about his intentions. 'What do you mean by that nonsense about sharin' the reward? You're the one that captured Rutherford. I didn't have nothin' to do with it. It's yours.'

'You're wrong, my friend. You did a lot when you received us so kindly when I was here before and again yesterday. You did young Carla a power of good by reminding her that there are decent folk around as well as those who did her so much wrong. I ain't got any family myself and you've got two lovely youngsters. I want you to have half the money to help you bring them up the way they deserve.' He hesitated and then, pretending a feigned warning, ordered an astonished Holiday to make sure his own share was kept safe until he returned to claim it later.

* * *

When William Grant returned to Plympton, he was warmly greeted by townsfolk who were all fully aware of his lone mission and were delighted when he told them that the missing gunman had been captured and was now safely behind bars.

Rutherford's accomplices at the cantina shootout had all been buried in an unpretentious plot away from the town's main graveyard.

Sam Grant had told Sheriff Goodrich the background to the events at the cantina as far as he had witnessed them, but was unable to provide details of the gunfight involving his uncle at the front of the building. Mr Hawkins had been able to confirm visually that Rutherford's two dead gang members were the men involved in the murder of his wife, though he was unable to name them. No one had bothered to identify which body had been buried in each of the six graves, however, and they remained unmarked, as had the remains of many lawbreakers in this age of violence in the Western territories.

There was one exception, though, when William later insisted that there should be a separate marker for the man in black. He asked the undertaker to erect a discreet tablet, bearing the words he personally provided: 'Englishman Hank, from Cornwall. Travelled far across the sea to live and die a real man in a new world'.

One man who was not best pleased at the way things had turned out, however, was the County Sheriff, Mike Goodrich. When news reached him that William Grant had returned alone, after depositing his captive with another lawman, the irate sheriff rode immediately to Plympton to challenge him.

'What the hell you playin' at?' he

demanded. 'I ordered you to bring Rutherford back to me if you captured him. You were actin' as my deputy. You needn't think you're claiming the full bounty reward 'cause you were acting as a lawman under my authority.'

'I don't know what the matter is with you, Sheriff — though I think I can guess. I suspected you somehow wanted in on the deal when I refused to go in with your plan to send out a posse. Let me remind you that no Texan lawman has any authority over the river, so what I did down there was off my own initiative. You ain't got no part in it.'

Goodrich practically exploded. 'You had my badge. You was actin' for me,' he argued angrily. 'You got no right to resign.'

'Actually, Sheriff, I didn't really need to. If you recall, you never got round to swearing me in. Just gave me the badge, so I was never a proper legal deputy anyway. But if you're concerned about the reward, you needn't bother yourself. I've already claimed it and am

180

sharin' it with someone who has never worn a badge in his life.'

William started to turn his back but then, with a huge grin on his face, looked round at the red-faced sheriff and added a parting shot before walking away. 'Suppose, though, that I ought to thank you for the loan of the horse. Fine animal. You'll find it in the livery stable, with payment in the saddle-bag.'

One other task for William was to tell Carla what had happened. She listened silently and carefully with an expression which her father and William assumed reflected unbounded hatred. Surprisingly, however, she eventually gave a deep sigh, which sounded more like relief rather than any other emotion.

'Yep, he was the one who took me away from my pa and brother. But he didn't do nothin' to me — not in the cantina or later. It was the others that violated me and they're all dead now, so I guess I've already got revenge for what they done. That's what I'll say at Rutherford's trial.'

20

Whilst they were eating a meal back in Crown Creek, William and Sam had two visitors.

'Oh no! Not you again!' said William when he saw the *Chicago Tribune* journalist, Pennington-Jones. 'What do you want now? And who's this?'

The journalist did not immediately introduce his companion, a girl of about twenty years of age, who was dressed in somewhat shabby riding gear. Instead, he doffed his hat and smiled ingratiatingly in response to William's challenge.

'Sorry to bug you, Marshal, but news travels fast these days, and we heard that the town marshal from Crown Creek had gone on a mission to rescue a young girl who had been captured by a gang of ruffians. I'm told you were then involved in a shootout in which several men were killed. Is that all true, Marshal?'

'Guess so,' grunted William, 'but let me tell you again that my business ain't your business. And I ain't a marshal no more, so you can stop callin' me that. And you still haven't told me who this young lady is. I thought you lot were supposed to have good manners.'

'No need for him to tell you, Marshal,' cut in the girl. 'My name's Kate Purvis.'

'Purvis?' It was Sam who responded first.

'Yes, Purvis. You recognize the name? I'm told the marshal should. He killed my two brothers, Clint and then James. One in Fort Worth and one in Crown Creek.'

She spat out the accusation with venom, but got no immediate response. William and Sam exchanged meaningful glances, both of them wondering if this was yet another member of the family set on revenge.

But they didn't need to respond to

the girl's accusation because the news-paperman hastened to correct her. 'No. We got that wrong at first. I've now been told it wasn't the marshal who killed your younger brother James here in Crown Creek.'

'Nope, he tried to kill *me*,' said William. 'Shot me in the shoulder. Still pains me sometimes,' he complained.

But the newspaperman wanted to push on with the story. 'I'm told it was another young fella who killed James.' He turned to Sam. 'Was that you?' he asked.

Before Sam could respond William held up his hand to silence his young partner. 'It's all on record,' he said to the girl. 'All came out in court, so don't you get any strange ideas of revenge like your brother did. Sam here didn't do wrong, so don't get any silly ideas like your kin.'

Suddenly the girl's demeanour changed. From her initial challenging attitude, she seemed to move into a mood near to distress.

'*You* killed him?' she asked Sam. 'Why?'

Sam hesitated, recalling the events with mixed emotions. 'It was instinctive,' he explained before going on to relate the disturbing story of the young man's death, and ending with an obviously heartfelt, but insufficient, apology to the distressed girl. 'I'm so sorry it ended that way,' he said, 'but your brother had evil intent. I saw him shoot the marshal in the street and thought he had killed him. So I shot him as he rode on.'

The girl broke into tears. 'James wasn't evil,' she sobbed. 'Clint wasn't really bad, either. It was just everything seemed to go wrong after our pa died. Clint couldn't face up to the hard work and poor returns of running our small farm. He took to the road and we heard that he got up to bad things and became wanted by the law. Then his body was returned to us with a message that he had been killed in Fort Worth by a lawman. I guess that was you, Mr Grant?'

'Yep, it was me. Young fella drew on me when I tried to arrest him. Had no choice. It was him or me.'

The girl nodded. 'That's what we heard but my brother James just couldn't accept it. Said he was gonna get the man who gunned down Clint. I pleaded with him not to be foolish but his character seemed to change. He wouldn't listen to reason. Now he's dead, too, and I've got nothing — not even the homestead. My ma and me left it because we couldn't manage it on our own, and my ma died within weeks of James riding off. I'm sure her heart was broken and she just couldn't carry on.'

There was a long silence after her outpouring, with no one knowing what to say. The journalist, though, had been busy scribbling in his notebook.

William turned to him. 'Don't know what you've been writin', but that's somethin' nearer the truth than that trash stuff some of you fellas write.

Many people travel out West with romantic ideas about a good life in open spaces, or riches from finding gold, or even ranching. What they often find is hardship, insanitary conditions, or even death — like Kate's two brothers. And, of course, some take the wrong road and end up as thieves, or even murderers, with dime novel writers often making them into heroes. But make no mistake. In the end right will win over wrong, even out here.'

It was the most philosophical speech Sam had ever heard from his uncle and William's obvious strength of feeling left his listeners silently reflecting on his words, with even the journalist holding his peace.

*   *   *

The following day Sam told Kate that it was his uncle who had arranged for her brother's burial in Crown Creek. They were walking together some way from the main town with Sam anxious to do

187

whatever he could to soften the hurt the girl was feeling and persuade her that his own actions had not been a deliberate act of malice against her younger brother.

They stood silently by a small stream and Sam expressed his regret at what had happened when young James had arrived in Crown Creek intent on revenge for Clint's death.

'I think there's something in the Bible about an eye for an eye or a tooth for a tooth but he was wrong to take the law into his own hands,' he said, turning to the girl who stood beside him.

His mouth dropped open in shock, though, when he saw Kate had a derringer pointed at him.

'Yes, that's right,' she said, 'an eye for an eye. It's what killers deserve. A bullet for a bullet, and all the fancy talk don't change the fact that you killed my brother. That newspaperman told me all what he had found out and reckoned that the law would be on my side if I put that wrong to right. He gave me this gun and said that no one would blame me if I shot my brother's killer. He suggested that perhaps the law should have done the job in the first place, instead of leavin' you a free man.'

She stood with the weapon pointed at Sam's chest, but took no further action as he looked her in the eye. He was shocked at the reversal of her previous friendlier attitude and her sudden decision to threaten him.

He was totally undecided about how to act but after many long seconds of silence, Kate's hand started to tremble. She murmured, 'But I can't do it. Killin' a man just ain't in my nature. There's been too much killin' already.'

Slowly, gently, Sam reached out, meaning to take the weapon from her shaking hand. He took a step toward her but as he moved closer, the weapon fired. At point blank range, its lethal effect was not in doubt. Sam's eyes rolled in pain and disbelief as his body slid to the ground at Kate's feet.

21

Three months passed before Sam's body was found by a courting couple who had been walking down by the creek.

Kate Purvis and the newspaperman had disappeared and the general assumption had been that Sam must have left town with them, though William had found it hard to accept that his nephew would have left without explaining his decision. Could he really have been so taken with the girl that he had decided to leave with her so hastily? And had she so fully forgiven him for killing her brother that she had accepted him as a friendly companion? Or could they have already formed an even closer relationship which caused them to leave Crown Creek without communicating their intentions?

Until his body was found, Sam's

disappearance had remained a mystery and William sank into a despondent mood as he was forced to accept that, this time, it was external circumstances — rather than his own actions — which had left him as a loner with no family and little interest in the shape of his future life.

★　★　★

'Suppose you want your old job back, William, now you're alone?' John Jenkins had been installed as the temporary town marshal while William had been off on his rescue mission. He sounded resentful at the idea that his predecessor might want to replace him now that his nephew was dead.

'No, John. I resigned. The job's yours now. I wish you luck with getting elected full time.'

'What are you goin' to do?'

'Nothing special. I'm going back to the family smallholding. As you know, it's been looked after by a neighbour, but it's mine now, I guess. I've got terrible memories of my brother and his wife being murdered there but I think Brett and Debra would probably approve of me settling in their home.'

★   ★   ★

But it was a lifestyle which William again acknowledged didn't really suit him. After a year, in which he mostly stayed in isolation, he handed the property back to the neighbour, moved back into lodgings in the town and surprised everyone by taking on construction work on the courthouse, using skills he hadn't known he possessed but working without any kind of real enthusiasm. The mystery surrounding his nephew's death had never been solved and it had clearly upset him to such an extent that he had become difficult to relate to. The man who had once been the respected and well-liked town marshal was now virtually ignored by his fellow citizens and that seemed to be the way he wanted it to remain.

His drinking had become more regular, with him frequently sitting alone in the Lucky Horseshoe. One evening he was in the saloon when he was approached by a familiar figure.

'Marshal Grant, you might remember me.'

'Sure, I do. You're that newspaper guy I gave short shrift to way back. Told you then that I hold no love for you busybodies poking your noses into other people's business.'

'I know that, Marshal, but — '

'I ain't the marshal no more, so get your facts right.'

'Sorry, *Mister* Grant, but I've got some news that I think will interest you.'

'The only news I want from you, fella, is what you can tell me about the death of my nephew, Sam. I've always had the suspicion that you and that Purvis girl were somehow involved in it. You disappeared without explanation at about the time he must have been killed. Did you have anything to do with it and what do you want now? Get to the point or get out of my face.'

Unabashed, the journalist went to the barman and got William's empty glass replenished before joining him at the table.

'Mr Grant, I certainly had nothing to do with the killing of your nephew, Sam. I had every reason to be in his debt.'

'How come?'

'Well, it was your nephew who gave me all the details of your exciting rescue of that young girl down in Mexico. I wrote it all down and don't mind telling you I made a packet of money by selling your riveting tale. Hope you don't mind but I changed your name slightly in my story because I figured you might not take kindly to being identified as some kind of hero. I called you Billy Grant, not William. Somehow seemed more appropriate. Is that OK?'

'Yep, guess so, but I still want to

know why you and that Kate girl disappeared from Crown Creek so suddenly. Folk seemed to assume that young Sam had gone with you — until we found his body, that is.'

'Yes, I know he was found in the bushes down by the water. I was very sorry to hear it. But I'll answer your question. We left Crown Creek suddenly because the girl came to me in a bad emotional state and begged me to take her away immediately. I had no reason to stay, so I agreed. I took her as far as Fort Worth and she caught the stage. Said she was heading for California, though she was acting rather cagey and I'm not sure that she was telling the truth. I don't really know where she and her two brothers originally came from but I seem to remember she once said something about Kansas.'

William sank his whiskey in one gulp and again challenged the newsman with the half-formed suspicion which had been in his mind ever since Sam's body had been found. 'Do you think that Purvis girl had anything to do with my nephew's death? It seemed they were linking up together after she said she accepted that Sam was acting properly when he killed her brother. But maybe that was just a ruse. Could she have killed him, or perhaps paid someone else to do it?'

Pennington-Jones paused before answering, and signalled for a full bottle of whiskey to be brought to them.

Topping up his glass, William changed the direction of his quizzing. 'OK — let's say that you and the girl had nothing to do with Sam's death. So why are you back here now? What's this news you said you have? I'll warn you, it had better be worthwhile. I'll not be best pleased if you are wasting my time again.'

'No, sir, I don't think you'll consider it a waste of your time if I tell you that I know where your Scotsman Mac-Donald is now.'

William plonked his glass down

noisily, and then picked it up again to fill it whilst he took in what the newsman had just said. 'What do you mean by saying where he is *now*. Isn't he still in that Mexican lair of his? And how would you know anything about him? Out with it, man.'

Knowing he had his listener's full attention, Pennington-Jones savoured his moment before revealing his news. 'Well it's a surprising story. He certainly isn't in Mexico any longer, I promise you that!'

'Well, where the devil is he? Surely he's not back this side of the border?'

'I know where he is, but I'm not prepared to tell you that. Not yet, anyway.'

'Don't play games with me, fella. How do you know where he is?'

'I know because I've been given such detailed information that I'm sure that what I've been told must be true. Someone read my account of your rescue mission and contacted me to say that MacDonald is back this side of the

Rio Grande, though using a different name. My informant has seen him and swears he matches the description Sam gave me and which I then put in my story. It all fits, right down to the picture of him in the Highlands of Scotland. He even described the fact that the man in the painting is wearing a kilt, which is what they call those skirt things.'

'So where's this picture?'

'It's hanging behind a bar in a saloon, which MacDonald apparently bought a few months back.'

'He bought a saloon? What saloon? Which town? I sure hope you're not playing games with me, fella. You'll regret it if you are, I promise you that! What town are we talking about?'

'Sorry, Mr Grant, but I'm not ready to tell you that — not yet, anyway. My guess is that you might want to go and see for yourself. Am I right?'

'Too *true*, you're right! Nothing I would like to do more than meet up with that man again.'

'That's exactly what I expected, but there's one other thing you might want to know . . . '

'What's that?'

'I'm told there's a woman with him. Sounds almost certain that it's the stunner Sam told me they called La Condesa. Does that interest you, Marshal?'

William absorbed this extra bit of news with what he admitted to himself was much more than just passing interest, but he covered his emotion by chiding the newspaperman again. 'Stop playing games with me. So where is MacDonald?'

Knowing that he had hooked his prey, the newsman stated his terms.

'I won't tell you, sir, but I'll take you there if you agree for me to ride along with you. I've got a strong feeling that a meeting between the two of you will produce a real interesting story for my readers. They seem to be fascinated by what's going on out here.'

22

Less than forty-eight hours later, Crown Creek was far behind them as the two men rode further west towards the distant rocky mountains. To his companion's surprise, the newsman proved to be an extremely good horseman and they made rapid progress.

Pennington-Jones seemed to be remarkably confident that he knew the route they needed to be taking, but he would still not reveal any detail about their final destination. This was despite being constantly questioned by his companion — a man who had clearly shaken off the lethargy which had settled over him since the death of Sam, his last surviving family member.

As they approached a town unknown to William despite all his previous travels, the newsman surprised him by reining in his mount, pointing at the buildings ahead and declaring that this was where they would find MacDonald.

'Well let's get at it,' declared an eager-sounding William. But he was restrained by his guide.

'No, let's leave it for now. I think we should get some rest tonight and ride in tomorrow. We don't know what we might face if MacDonald has still got some of his henchmen with him. Given your past history with him, he may not give us too friendly a welcome. And, anyway, I want you to tell me exactly what you intend to do when you confront him.'

'Guess you might be right, fella. We'll go in tomorrow. Let's hope your information is correct. It had better be.'

As they drank their coffee, William attempted to answer the newsman's question. 'To be truthful, I don't know what I'll do. I suppose it depends on what he says, and how he acts. It's always been my policy to let the law decide what should happen to those who've broken the rules. I've made it

201

my job to bring them in alive, rather than punish them.'

Pennington-Jones acknowledged the truth behind this remark. 'Yes, I was particularly impressed that you handed Rutherford over to the authorities, when you had every chance to finish him off. Weren't you tempted to kill the man who murdered your family?'

'Sure I was tempted, but the fact is that he denied carrying out the murders at my brother's place. As he travelled back as my prisoner he told me lots of things. He boasted about various crimes he had committed. I don't know whether he was trying to impress me or scare me, but all he actually did was give me a great deal of detailed information I could pass on to the authorities.

'The important thing to me, though, was that he claimed it wasn't him that killed Brett, Debra and little Annie during their raid on our family homestead. He said it was one of his men and he actually apologized for what had happened. He said he tried to stop the killing on that awful day, and I believed him. So it wasn't personal.'

'But what about MacDonald, then? Is that personal? And what do you intend to do?'

'We'll see,' was the only answer Pennington-Jones got.

23

As soon as they stepped into the Silver Blade Saloon, it was obvious that there had been no mistake. The information the newsman had received was accurate, because hanging prominently behind the bar was the painting that Pennington-Jones had described and that William remembered clearly from the Glencoe hideout.

Early in the day there were few customers in the saloon. The two newcomers attracted no more than casual attention as they ordered beers. They surveyed the room but remained standing at the bar until William could contain himself no longer.

'Where's MacDonald?' he demanded.

The barman had no need to reply, because one of the drinkers overheard the question. He stood up and walked towards William and the newsman.

'Ain't no one here going by that name. So who are you? And what do you want?'

'What I want, fella, is to meet up with that rogue in the painting up there. If you know the answer to my question you best decide to be more helpful — and keep your hand away from that revolver. I think I recognize you from down in Mexico and you might remember me. Right?'

The man did not respond but a nervous glance up the stairs leading to an upper floor gave William the information he needed. He pulled his Colt from its holster and indicated that the man should lead the way up the stairs. Reluctantly, MacDonald's henchman did so, persuaded by the weapon pressed into his back. At the top of the stairs, he stopped and rapped at a closed door.

'Who's that?' came angrily from inside.

'It's Merton, sir. You've got a visitor.'

As the man spoke, William turned the door handle and pushed Merton inside ahead of him. He was also conscious that Pennington-Jones was pressing behind him.

'*I'm your visitor*, MacDonald. You'll remember me. I caused you a bit of bother down in Mexico.' Shoving Merton aside as he spoke, William now levelled his .45 at the man seated behind an imposing desk. In what was almost a replica of the scene in the Mexican hideout, the girl known as La Condesa was sat in a chair in the corner of the room.

She had apparently been reading a sheaf of what looked like some kind of official document. She put this to one side as she stared at William in a direct appraisal, a penetrating examination which immediately made him feel more than a little conscious of her. As before, he felt an unspoken bond which he would have found impossible to explain.

MacDonald had seemingly recovered from his initial shock after the men had pushed into his office. 'Of course I remember you. Called yourself Ross but then we found out that wasn't your real name. Isn't that right?'

'Yep, that's right. You found out by taking the whip to poor Alberto Lopez. Thrashed him to death, is what I was told. Reckon you ought to hang for that.'

'You're joking, man. No jury is going to find me guilty of something that happened in Mexico when there aren't even any witnesses. You weren't there so what you say doesn't count for anything.'

Unexpectedly, there was an interruption from the corner of the room. A cultured female voice with a beguiling Spanish accent cut into MacDonald's defence. 'You're wrong there. I witnessed the whole thing. I saw what you did to that poor man. You killed him even though he was clearly telling you the truth.'

There was a look of surprised shock on MacDonald's face as he turned to look at the woman.

'Maybe. But you won't be saying anything if you know what's good for you!'

'You could be very wrong there,' she replied to his challenge. 'Perhaps this is just what I've been waiting for all this time you've had me as your captive, regarding me as no more than a piece of furniture, with me always knowing that you would order the killing of my mother back in Mexico if I made any kind of move against you. But I'm tired of being your toy. Perhaps now's the time for me to break away from you.'

'You wouldn't dare! You know the consequences,' snarled MacDonald.

'There are no consequences. What you don't know is that I received a message telling me that my poor mother has died, so there's nothing you can threaten me with any more.'

MacDonald was about to reply, but there was a shout from Pennington-Jones. 'Marshal, look out.'

William spun round just in time to see that Merton had got his pistol out of his holster, but two quick bullets in the chest from the Colt, which was already in his hand, dropped the henchman, whose weapon clattered to the floor, followed more slowly by the man's body.

That wasn't the end of the action, however. Whilst William was distracted, MacDonald dived at the woman. He had a vicious dirk in his hand. He dragged her out of her chair and twice plunged the blade into her stomach; blood immediately spurted out from the wounds.

Enraged by the sight, William flung himself at the Scot and grabbed him round the throat. It took several minutes of struggling and choking before MacDonald's body finally capitulated and — possibly — his soul returned to Scotland.

As William pushed the man's dead body to one side, he heard a whispered request from the woman he only knew as La Condesa. 'Hold me,' she begged. 'Please hold me.'

Those five words were the only ones she had ever addressed to William and he realized that he had never spoken a single word to her. But as he cradled her in his arms he felt an unbelievable closeness. It was an emotion as powerful as the feelings he had once had for his brother's wife, Debra, all those years ago.

In the short time he held the dying Spanish beauty close to him he felt that some kind of strange destiny had brought him to this point of such strong attachment. She smiled up at him as she expelled her last breath. He continued to hold her and — despite his anguish — also sensed some kind of exhilaration. He somehow knew that his presence had been as important to her, as it was to him. That certain knowledge gave him a satisfaction he would carry with him for the rest of his life.

Epilogue

Subsequently, Pennington-Jones got a lot more than just a single story from the day's dramatic events. His reporting skills, spiced with just a modicum of artistic elaboration, earned him plaudits galore — and a very satisfying income.

His major advantage was that he, alone, was the only witness to the dramatic action in the Silver Blade Saloon. Under the prominent front page headline, TEXAS JUSTICE, he was able to fulfil the reporter's dream of describing a real-life story which he could present as a personal account.

In a room above a Texas saloon bar, I witnessed a drama of violence and retribution in which two men and a beautiful woman all lost their lives in a matter of only a couple of minutes. A Colt revolver, a vicious knife and an ex-marshal's strong hands around an enemy's throat were all involved in a scene which I could never have imagined even if I was writing a piece of fiction.

His report told the back history of all the events before the final shocking moments which concluded with William Grant comforting a dying woman cradled in his arms. The newsman was able to recount his previous reported story of the Mexican mercy mission. Then he went on to claim personal credit for leading the hero of that earlier event to the final fatal meeting with the Scot, who had organized and run the hideout protecting so many notorious criminals.

He described the deaths of Merton, MacDonald and La Condesa in breathless prose, which was lapped up first by his editors and then by a public more than ready to vicariously experience a way of life, and death, so far removed from their own.

A few weeks later his eager readers were able to learn more as he reported the court case in which he had revelled in the role of chief witness, re-telling the story in vivid detail. Throughout his testimony he carefully exonerated William Grant from all blame, even though the defendant had admitted that he had killed two people. The sympathetic jury would later agree it was justifiable action.

The trial itself was not long and William was free to continue a life which somehow felt less empty, despite the physical loss of his family and the woman he had never spoken to but who had inexplicably meant so much to him. Surprisingly, no one laid any claim to her, despite the wide coverage of her death, and William was allowed to take her body back to the family homestead near Crown Creek, where she was laid to rest close to the graves of his mother, father, brother and sister-in-law, as well as his niece and nephew.

With commendable discretion, Pennington-Jones decided not to write anything about William's actions following the trial, even though he knew that he had revisited the Holiday family to collect his share of the bounty money, and had then used some of this to repay the neighbour who had been taking care of the family homestead.

Crown Creek townsfolk who knew of William Grant's history were surprised to find that he now appeared to be ready to settle there in what seemed to be something akin to contented early retirement.

To avoid the danger that the town and the Grant homestead might become a site of morbid public curiosity, Pennington-Jones made no reference to it in his writings and the town's ex-marshal was left in peace, although he had made it clear that he was always ready to help if his successor as town marshal, John Jenkins, needed any extra support.

In any case, Pennington-Jones had other priorities. First, he was contacted by a number of people who recognized Ian MacDonald from the reports of the trial. Using this information, he was able to produce several authenticated stories about the Scot's notorious past. The man's crimes included treasonable action against former army colleagues, theft of army property and gun-running down into Mexico, with a couple of murders along the way.

Impressed by the sales created by this juicy reporting, his editors gave him a generous commission to travel down to Mexico in order to see what he could find out about the Scotsman's activities south of the border. In particular, he was to investigate the background of the mysterious woman known simply as La Condesa.

Before he left, the newsman took the trouble to contact William in order to offer him the opportunity to join in the journey south, thinking he might be keen to learn for himself how Mac-Donald had come to have her as his prisoner. He was turned down flat, however.

'I know all I need to,' was the response he got. 'I followed your lead before, because there was something that needed doing, but I'm not interested in the past. You go and do your investigating yourself this time. I'm staying here in Crown Creek.'

As he set off alone, Pennington-Jones reflected that his Texas story-telling had started when he had found out about a young man's intention to revenge his brother's Fort Worth death at the hands of a marshal. This had then led to an even more exciting story about an amazingly successful attempt to rescue an abducted young girl from a bandit hideout. And being a witness to the final dramatic episode in the Silver Blade Saloon had been a reporter's godsend.

Now he hoped that the trip down

into Mexico might mean that he could perhaps add a complete new dimension to the saga, though he was sensitive enough to acknowledge that anything he discovered was unlikely to be of practical benefit to the various protagonists whose histories his pen had recorded.

All in all, the Chicago-based journalist had many reasons to be pleased with himself as he set off on his long journey, but as he travelled south from Chicago, there was a strongly worrying sense of guilt he could not erase from his thoughts.

He carried with him the troubling knowledge that he had been the one to give Kate Purvis the derringer, which he now felt certain had killed Sam Grant. When she had pleaded with him to get her away from Crown Creek in haste he had been unaware that Sam lay dead in the bushes. She hadn't confessed to the crime but when he now reflected on her emotional state he was convinced that she had taken the young man's life.

That, however, was a part of the saga he would never report — one which must ever remain hidden from William Grant.